A SINGLE TOUCH

W WINTERS

Copyright © 2019 by Willow Winters All Rights Reserved.

No part of this publication may be reproduced, stored in a retrieval system, or transmitted in any form or by any means, electronic, mechanical, photocopying, recording, scanning, or otherwise, without the prior written permission of the publisher, except in the case of brief quotations within critical reviews and otherwise as permitted by copyright law.

NOTE: This is a work of fiction.

Names, characters, places, and incidents are a product of the author's imagination.

Any resemblance to real life is purely coincidental. All characters in this story are 18 or older.

Copyright © 2019, Willow Winters Publishing. All rights reserved. willowwinterswrites.com

From *USA Today* bestselling author W. Winters comes the conclusion to the breathtaking, heart-wrenching romantic suspense trilogy, Irresistible Attraction.

Sometimes you meet someone, although maybe *meet* isn't quite the right word. You don't even have to say hello for this to happen. You simply pass by them and everything in your world changes forever. Chills flow from where you imagine he'd kiss you in the crook of your neck, moving all the way down with only a single glance.

I know you know what I'm referring to. The moment when something inside of you ignites to life, recognizing the other half that's been gone for far too long.

It burns hot, destroying any hope that it's only a coincidence, and that life will go back to what it was. These moments are never forgotten.

That's only with a single glance.

I can tell you what a single touch will do. It will consume you and everything you thought you knew.

I felt all of this with Jase Cross, with every flicker of the flames that roared inside of me.

I knew he'd be my downfall, and I was determined to be his just the same.

A Single Touch is **the third and final** book of the Irresistible Attraction trilogy.
A Single Glance and *A Single Kiss* must be read first.

"Past is a nice place to visit,
but certainly not a good place to stay."
—Anonymous

A SINGLE TOUCH

PROLOGUE

Bethany

MY CALCULUS GRADES ARE SLIPPING. THE large red D scribbled in Miss Talbot's handwriting stares back at me. One look at it shoves the knot in the back of my throat even deeper down my windpipe. My bookbag falls to the floor in the nursing home with a dull thud as I whisper the word, "fuck." With my hand rubbing under my tired eyes, I let out a heavy sigh and stare at the ceiling in the hallway.

There's no way I'm going to be able to stay in college if I don't pass. There's no coming back from this. My grades didn't slip like this last year when Jenny was here with me every day at four o'clock on the dot. I only have one more year to go, but this class is a core requirement. I'll never need to know how the hell derivatives work in order to be a nurse, but I can't fail this class. I can't fucking fail.

"Bethany?" The soft voice belongs to Nurse Judy. She told me exactly how she got her degree and that I could do it just *like she did. She's the reason I changed my major sophomore year to pursue a nursing degree. Just as she creeps into the long hall, I shove the test into a notebook while stuffing it into my worn leather backpack, listening to the sound of the zipper rather than what she's saying.*

I'll fail calculus, lose the scholarship that's paid for more than half of my college education, and be left with even more debt and no degree to show for it. Perfect. I don't know what I'm going to do. Other than work a nine-to-five at whatever minimum wage job I can get. If they'll even hire me.

"Did you hear me?" Nurse Judy coaxes me out of my downward spiral and it's then that I see the worried look in her dark brown eyes. "Your mother had a relapse."

"A relapse?" The confusion leaves a deep crease on my forehead.

"We don't know what caused it, but she's with us, Bethany. Mentally aware."

"Aware?" All the air leaves me with the single word.

"She woke up, not knowing what happened during the last three or so years. But she knows time has passed. She knows you and your sister have been on your own and that she has Alzheimer's."

"I don't understand how that's possible." Fear is something I never expected to feel in this moment. I've had so many dreams come to me in the middle of the night where my mother would be lucid. Where she'd tell me it was okay, that she was back now. Back for good and that she remembers everything. They were only dreams though. It's only ever a dream.

I can barely swallow as I stare past Nurse Judy and walk forward without conscious awareness. "Is she okay?" It's the only thing I can ask. I can't imagine what it's like to wake up one day to have lost years of time. To wake up and find your children look different and everything's changed.

The oddest thing in this moment is that I hope she still loves me. I just want her to love me still.

Even if I'm failing. Even if I'm no longer her little girl. It's been years since she's been lucid and this is what I want most of all.

"She'll be better when she sees you," is the answer Nurse Judy gives me. With each step, I know I'll always remember this moment. It's like something flipped a switch in my head and a voice gives me reassurance. This moment will never leave you. This moment will define you.

"Are they here?" my mother's voice calls out. Echoed in her voice, I can hear the strain of past tears. "Did they get your messages?"

My answer drowns out Nurse Judy's as I round the corner to the living room in the home, my steps picking up pace just as my throat tightens. "Mom," I croak.

She's frail and thin, as she was yesterday and the day before. Somehow I thought when she came into view, she'd look like she did the last time I held her hand and she asked me again who my sister was.

She had her makeup done perfectly although she didn't need it. Mom used to say she'd never grow old. Even joked about it that day as she brushed her blush up to her temples. That was the day we took her to the hospital. She'd forgotten who my sister was and it took me a long time to realize she'd forgotten who I was too. She thought I was her best friend from high school, the girl she named me after. A girl who had long since died.

My mother squeezes me harder today than she did back then and the tickle in the back of my throat grows impatient as I hold my breath and squeeze her back just as tight.

I don't cry until her body wracks with sobs against mine. "Sorry," she tells me. "I'm so sorry," is all she can say over and over.

As if she chose this. As if she wanted to forget the life she had and let the memories fade and die. That's what forgetting is, it's the death of the life you had. It doesn't just kill you though. It kills everyone else as well.

I only pull away from her for a moment, just to tell her there's nothing to be sorry for, but the words are lost when she looks into my eyes. Her own are gray and clouded with a gaze of sorrow.

"Mom?"

Her expression changes in an instant. Confusion clouds her face, where just minutes ago there was clarity.

My mother is in there, or she was, but the moment is gone.

"Who are you?"

"Mom, come back," I beg her, feeling my chest hollow and then fill with agony. "Where'd you go?" I ask her, not giving into the fear this time, only the loss. "Mom!" Hope is undeniable. "I'm here, Mom; I'm here!"

Her hand tightens on my forearm, too tight.

"Mom," I gasp, trying to pry her hands off of me as she refuses to look away, refuses to react to anything at all. She's merely a statue and the realization frightens me. I turn to look over my shoulder just as I hear the front door shut from the hall. My heartbeat races. Where'd Nurse Judy go?

"Mom," I protest, writhing out of her grasp. "Help!" I finally call out, the fear winning.

"Everyone I loved has died," my mother says, and her voice is ragged. Despair and loss morph her features into one of pain and her grip on me loosens.

Staring into my eyes with sincerity, she tells me, "Everyone you love will die before you do." As if she's talking to a stranger she only intends to bring pain, they're the last words she speaks before her slender body relaxes into the chair. Her gaze wanders aimlessly as I stand there breathless from both fear and despair, knowing I was too late. That's when I hear the quickened footsteps of my sister running into the room.

Running to see her mother. Who's already gone.

Seconds pass, and I can't look at Jenny. I brush the tears away as Nurse Judy pushes past us both, aiding my mother, whose consciousness has drifted to another place and another time.

"Mom," my sister cries. And I don't blame her.

That was the last time my sister cried for our mother. She didn't even cry at her funeral nearly a year later. Jenny always held it against her that our mother didn't wait for her. She held it against me too, knowing I at least got to hear Mom tell me she was sorry.

I never told her what else our mother said. I tried to forget it. I did everything I could to kill that memory.

It's come back though. It refuses to die, unlike other things in my life.

Chapter 1

Bethany

THE CLOCK DOESN'T STOP TICKING.
It's one of those simple round clocks. There's nothing special about the white backing and thick black frame. *Tick, tick, tick.* It's loud and unforgiving. The torture of it is all I can focus on to bring me sanity as the last hours of my life fall like dominoes in my memory.

The money in the trunk.

"You still haven't explained where you got the three hundred thousand dollars." Officer Walsh's voice is hard.

The blood on Jase's clothes and the look in his eyes when I came into his bathroom.

"Or why you were covered in blood. Whose blood is it, Miss Fawn? You need to tell us."

Fear is what motivated me to run from him. Fear is the cause of all of this. It's left me now, though. In its place is something more resigned.

One long, deep breath falls from me as I stare at the painted white bricks of the interrogation room's walls and listen to the *tick, tick, tick.*

My piss-poor decisions have led to this point in my life.

The point of waiting. I've fucked it up enough; I may as well just let it all fall. When Alice fell, she landed in Wonderland. I'm thinking that's not where I'll land, but I'm ready to feel the weightlessness of what's to come. I'm simply tired of fighting it.

There's another officer in the room. He's younger. When I first listened to their demands for me to answer their questions, I sat here hours ago with my shoulders tense and feeling the need to curl up into a ball and hide. The young cop sat across from me, his arms crossed and his gaze never wandering from me.

I don't like him or the way he looks at me.

"We're doing a DNA test now. You think it's going to hit, Walsh?" The other officer, Linders, finally speaks to Walsh, even if his eyes are still pinned on me. There's a certain level of disdain that seeps into my skin every time I meet his gaze.

"I'll tell you what I think," Officer Walsh answers. He's staring at me too, even as he taps the stack of papers in his hand and continues, "I think she was in the wrong place at the wrong time and that she has names."

Tick, tick, the clock goes on. It's been like this for hours in this cold interrogation room. An ache in my back reminds me how uncomfortable this metal chair is.

"I don't think so. I think she was hired for a hit or was hiring someone else and it went wrong." Officer Linders speaks clearly, although his voice is low and rough. "A hit or drugs. There's no other explanation. Who'd you get the cash from?" he asks me. It has to be the hundredth time they've asked about the cash. "Where did it all go wrong?"

"I already told you," I start to say but don't recognize my tired voice anymore as I lift my gaze to Officer Walsh's and then to Linders's. "I don't have anything to say."

Officer Walsh leans forward, exasperated. The metal legs grind against the floor as he repositions in his chair. "I saw how scared you were," he says. Compassion wraps itself around every word and his gaze pleads with me to give him something. "I can help you."

A second passes and then another.

I could let it all out. I could tell them the truth. I know I could. Maybe they'd give me a new name and send me off to some place where bad men can't find me. Somewhere free of all these memories. A place where I didn't have to think of my sister or my fucked up life.

Where I wouldn't feel the presence of Jase Cross on every inch of surface I can see, smell, touch.

As I swallow, the click of the the heat switching on is all that can be heard in the room.

I don't want to live in that world. In a world where Jase Cross doesn't hover over me. Even if he scared the hell out of me. Recalling the sight of him sitting there on the edge of the tub, tilting his head to look me in the eyes, makes me close mine tight. I don't know what happened, but I can't leave him.

More than anything, the incessant ticking of the clock reminds me that every second that passes, I'm not with him. He's not okay and I'm not with him.

Let me fall to whatever may await me, and I'll crawl my way back up to Jase. I'll find him or he'll find me. And when that happens, he better fucking confess. I deserve to know what happened.

Strands of my hair wind around my finger as I ignore Officer Walsh. He hasn't charged me yet, but I know he will. I'll be charged with obstruction of justice for not giving them information about the blood on my shirt when it comes back confirmed from a human... or maybe with a name. God forbid it comes back as from a missing person. And who knows what I'll be charged with because of the cash in the back of my car. I don't even know what the offenses will be, since so many have been listed off in their speculation of what I've done.

But I'll never say a word. And that's how I know I care more for Jase than I should. And why he needs to tell me *everything*.

"There's no helping anything. Whatever she says will be a lie." The dark stare of Officer Linders makes my stomach curl.

Good cop, bad cop, I suppose. I manage to offer him a hint of a smile. My mouth moves on its own and I didn't mean for it to do that. It just happens. As if I need to tempt fate any further.

"Let me make you an offer," Officer Walsh starts and Linders huffs in disdain, rocking back in the chair and for the first time his gaze shifts from me. He's young, very Italian in appearance although he doesn't have an accent. He scratches at his coarse dark stubble as Officer Walsh draws my attention.

"I used to work for the FBI and I have some friends in

town, looking into things." There's a sense of compassion and empathy in Cody Walsh's voice that's hypnotizing, like a lullaby that draws you in. "What I'm trying to tell you is that I have connections. I know what happened to your sister. I know Jase Cross has been seen at your residence."

His light blue eyes sharpen every time he says, 'Cross.' "What I know is that you can have a happy life. You can start over, Bethany. All you have to do is tell me what happened."

It's like he read my mind. A way out. This is the bottom of the barrel, isn't it? When you need witness protection to find a way out of the hole you've dug for yourself.

Officer Linders clears his throat and the spell from Walsh is broken for only a moment as my eyes flick between the two of them. A man with hate for me, and another who I've felt from the first day I saw him, that he wanted to help me.

"All you have to do is tell me what happened." His hand gestures an inch above the table as he adds, "No matter how guilty you may feel; no matter what you've done."

Everything seems to slow as a part of my conscience begs me to consider. The part that remembers how dark Jase's eyes were when I last saw him. The part that's fear's companion. The part that questions if I'm strong enough for all this. Even if Jase tells me what he did and why he was sitting there like that, like he was someone else. Even if I pretend as though what happened earlier today will never happen again.

And yet another part of me is like a signal amid all the noise. A part that's fading away. A small part that remembers this all started because I wanted a single thing from Jase Cross.

A name. The murderer who made the one person I had left in my life disappear. Justice for my sister.

A name Jase has yet to deliver.

I have to blink away the thoughts, and Officer Walsh seems to take it as me considering his offer.

Say nothing, do nothing. Say nothing, do nothing. Fall down the rabbit hole; they can even throw me in that pit if they want. When I finally land, I'll do what I've always done. I'll stand up on my own and keep moving. With Jase or without.

Three knocks at the door startle me, causing the chair I'm firmly seated in to jump back. Officer Walsh is the one to stand and rise, leaving Linders staring at me, relishing in the hint of fear I've shown. I can barely hear someone outside the slightly ajar door speaking to Officer Walsh over the sound of my heart racing.

All my life, I've lived by elementary rules. *Do what is right and not what is wrong.* It's the simplest way to break down the laws of life. And yet here I sit, not knowing my judgment and wondering when the black and white of right and wrong turned so gray for me. Especially since I can't even list all the wrong things I've done recently. There are too many to count, yet I'd defend them all.

"Be right back." Officer Walsh is tense as he grips the door, locks eyes with me, then leaves the room. With only Linders across from me, a new tension rises inside of me.

I don't like the way he looks at me. Fear and anger curl my fingers into a fist in my lap.

Say nothing, do nothing.

He stares at me and I him, neither of us saying a word until a small red light goes off to my left. It's oddly placed in between the painted bricks. If it had never come on, I would've never known of its existence. And the little red light changes everything.

"It's clear for the moment, but I don't know how long we'll have, so I'll be fast," Linders says quickly with a new tone I haven't heard from him. Leaning forward, the distaste vanishes, and the hate I felt he had for me is nowhere to be found.

"It's all being scrubbed; every shred of evidence on you is going to vanish. Or it already has. Officer Walsh won't have anything to hold you on and no charges will be pressed."

"What?" Disbelief takes the form of a whisper.

"He already knows someone here at the station is in their back pocket. It'll be all right," he assures me when my expression doesn't change. "If you want to go to a cell, tell me. If you'd rather stay here, we'll have to keep this up when Walsh comes back, but I'll make sure he doesn't cross the line. There are others too who are loyal to Walsh, but I'll stay with you the entire time. Unless you want to be alone."

"I don't understand." I don't know why that's my reply.

Because I do understand. The pieces line up with one another perfectly. The Cross brothers control the police department. I knew that. I know that now, even. But to be a part of it, to see it happening…

"Mr. Cross told me to protect you and get you out of here." His eyes search mine, although there isn't a bit of judgment to be found.

"Thank you," is all I can say although I wrap my arms around myself and contemplate what would have happened if I was in a different mindset. If I was ready to spill my guts. If I was wanting that new life Walsh sold me so well.

I should feel relief, which I do. The more nagging thoughts are of how powerful Jase is. How much damage a single man could do. And how little I know about him. Yet how willing I was to fall for him.

What if I had said something? What then?

"The shirt's been destroyed and that's really the only damaging piece he had on you," Linders tells me, clearing his throat.

The money.

"What about the money?" The question leaves me with haste just as the red light vanishes, blending in with the wall once again.

"Are you going to sit there and deny everything? Maybe I should put you behind bars and see how you like that," Linders sneers, forcing my body to turn ice cold. I can feel the blood drain from my face, even if I'm consciously aware this time that it's all an act.

"What's it going to be, Miss Fawn? Are you going to talk? Or do you want us to stick you in a cell like the criminal you are?" Those are the options he offers me as the door opens and Walsh returns. Walsh's demeanor is defeated as he motions for Linders to follow him out of the interrogation room.

Linders doesn't though. He doesn't obey the command from his superior. He waits for me, wanting to know an answer.

Words get stuck in my throat and I try to swallow them, I try to speak.

Nothing comes. Not a word is spoken as I stare into Linders' gaze, knowing he's one of so many men who do Jase's bidding.

Jase is still here, still in this room, protecting me even when I didn't know it.

CHAPTER 2

Jase

"It's risky with the FBI already involved," Seth speaks from the driver's seat as we're parked out front of the police station. His eyes seek mine out in the rearview mirror and I meet them, but I only nod, not bothering to speak. "Four men now, active agents, coming all the way down here from New York." He sucks his front teeth in the absence of a response from me.

It's all my fault. It's my fault she's in there. I know it is. What I don't know is what the fuck came over me.

A voice in the back of my head answers instantly. *She did*. Bethany Fawn came over me.

"We should prepare for someone to take the fall," Seth continues and a grunt of acknowledgment comes from my chest.

I've already been thinking about it. How best to handle this particular fuckup of mine. It involves a dead former FBI agent by the name of Cody Walsh and one of my men in a jail cell taking the fall. Judge Martin will give the minimum sentence. All because I fucked up at a time when fucking up isn't a possibility.

"Someone who needs the money for their family. Someone who'd go away for a year and be all right with that." Seth rattles on.

"Chris Mowers," I finally answer him and then clear my throat although my eyes stay glued to the double doors at the front entrance. "He's new to the crew, young and seemingly naïve. His dad isn't doing well. Medical costs and looking out for his mother while he's serving time should do it. Besides, we've primed him for this." Chris wanted to work for me. I told him to go through the police academy, to earn a position we could use to our advantage. "He's not going to like it. But we can make it worth it."

My answer receives a single nod from Seth followed by the impatient tapping of his foot in the front seat.

"You're too nervous," I comment. I'm well aware of the consequences and everything at stake in this moment. The nerves he feels are nothing compared to the turmoil rattling inside of me. "Knock it the fuck off."

With his hand running over his chin he takes in a deep breath, but doesn't speak. Instead he releases a long sigh.

"You have something on your mind?" I push him.

I start to think he's going to keep it from me, whatever it is he's thinking, and then he finally says, "She's different."

Bethany. Every muscle in my body tenses at the mere mention of her.

"Yes," I answer him, feeling a pressure inside of my chest that makes me grit my teeth.

"She's in your head." He swallows after speaking.

Narrowing my eyes, I answer him with an acknowledging yes.

"I don't know how to help that," Seth admits, breaking eye contact in the small rectangular mirror for the first time. I hear him readjust in the seat in front of me as he adds, "I don't know what I should have done differently." When I don't immediately respond to that, he doesn't say anything else.

The sound of a car driving past us intrudes on the silence and I watch the tires leave tracks on the asphalt after driving through a small puddle. The brutal cold hasn't stopped the early spring flowers from pushing through the dirt out front of the police station.

Staring at the double doors that hold my cailín tine behind them, I finally answer him, "This is all on me. I know where I fucked up and you did everything right."

"What if it happens again?" he questions and a coil of anger tightens inside of me. He adds, "What do you want me to do? When you took off, I knew I should have stopped you."

I don't have time to answer him. Instead my attention is drawn to the doors being held open by Curt Linders while Bethany walks through them. With her arms crossed, she stands at the top of the concrete stairs, looking smaller than she ever has to me. Her hair is wild as the wind blows from her left and it's then that her gaze lands on our car.

"You don't have to worry about it," I say without taking my eyes off of her. "The next time I'll be the one taking the fall," I answer him and push my door open, not hesitating to go to her. Curt's shock doesn't go unnoticed. Neither does Seth's protest to simply wait for her and for me to remain inside the vehicle.

Neither of them understand. At this point, all I want is to be seen with her.

Let them all see. They need to know she's mine.

I'm drawing the line here, hoping it keeps her beside me regardless of what happens.

Bethany manages to take two steps by the time I've closed the distance between us. She's hesitant even as I wrap my arm around the small of her back.

A sharp hammering in my chest beats faster than my shoes thud on the pavement to get her in my car and away from this situation.

The feeling of failing her, of her knowing and seeing who I truly am grips me and in turn, I hold her closer. I'll never forget the way she looked at me before running off.

"It was a mistake," I mutter beneath my breath, but the tension in her body doesn't lessen and she doesn't look up at me in the least.

Seth's quick to get out and open the door for us. I'm only grateful she doesn't pause before slipping inside.

The door shuts with a resounding click as another gust of wind blows.

"You all right?" Seth asks me and I look him dead in the eyes to answer him. "No more fucking questions."

I don't have the answers to give him. None that I'm willing to give, anyway.

The bitter cold from outside doesn't carry into the back of the car. The warmth is lacking nonetheless as we leave the police department behind in silence.

The dull hum of the car doesn't last long. "Nothing will happen to you. I promise you." My words are quiet, but I know she hears them.

Her hands stay in her lap and she answers while still looking out of her window, "Thank you."

I didn't expect this distance between us. I didn't expect the damage to be so obvious. Regret urges me closer to her, leaning across the leather seat to grip her chin between my thumb and forefinger and forcing her to look at me.

She doesn't resist, but uncertainty lingers in the depths of her hazel eyes and her breathing becomes unsteady.

"I'm sorry," I whisper. "I should never have let you see that."

She only swallows, the sound so loud in the quiet space between us.

"No, you shouldn't have. But I shouldn't have run."

"It would have been better if you hadn't." There's no fire, no fight, nothing except hurt. "I know it scared you."

It's the way she hesitates before answering. The strained way she breathes in when she looks into my eyes. *She doesn't trust me.*

"I don't know what to think right now. I'm going back and forth."

"Back and forth?"

"Whether or not I'm capable of standing beside you. Of demanding you tell me what the fuck happened." Her voice drops as she adds, "And whether or not I can stomach the truth."

It's been a long damn time since I've felt the sense of losing someone. Of feeling them slip through my fingers. I can feel it; I can fucking *see* it. I just don't know how to change it.

"Marry me." I let the idea slip out, but keep my composure. I can't lose her. I fucked up, but everyone fucks up at some point. She'll get over it. I just need time. "They can't make you testify if you're legally married to me." The excuse comes out easily enough.

Her eyes widen as I lean back in my seat. I thought about it every second we sat outside the department. She needs to be my wife.

"You're fucking crazy to think I'd take that proposal seriously."

"If something happens--"

"I'd go to jail," she cuts me off, her fire blazing as the irritation grows in her eyes. "I'd rather go to jail than marry someone because I accidentally saw something I shouldn't have." She eyes me as if I've lost it, and maybe I have. "I'll stick to my story that I don't know how any of it happened and I don't have anything else to say. Thank you very much," she says, and her final quip comes with the crossing of her legs away from me. She stares out the window again and it's then I realize where the term 'cold shoulder' comes from.

"I had a moment, Bethany. Don't hold this against me." My voice is calm and like a balm it visibly soothes her prickly demeanor.

She's slow to look over her shoulder, peeking at me before saying, "Everyone has moments, but it scared the fuck out of me, Jase."

"I'll apologize again, I'm sorry-"

"I don't want an apology." Her entire tone changes, and a different side of her I've never seen presents itself. She's calm, receptive, concerned even. "What the hell happened?"

I've never spoken about Angie to anyone so openly. Not even my brothers know all the details. Not Seth. No one.

I repeat forcefully, "I had a moment."

She pauses, considering me, but returns to the cold condition she had moments ago as she says, "I want to go home."

"No." I answer her with more force than I intended.

"Yes," she snaps back. "You can have your moment. But if you aren't going to tell me what the hell happened, I'm not going back to your place right now so I can have my own damn moment."

I shouldn't be so turned on by her anger.

"You still owe me twenty-seven days." I remind her of the only card I have to play, leaning closer and daring her to fight me. The tension in the car thickens and heats.

"Fuck you," she retorts far too casually, pulling the sleeves of the large white sweater she was given in the department down her arms. It's a simple plain sweatshirt material, and it does nothing to show off her figure. I had Linders offer it to her since her own shirt was confiscated… and now incinerated back at The Red Room like it should have been initially. Before she ran.

"Did you forget about our deal?"

She ignores my question and replies, "I had three hundred thousand in cash in the back of my car."

"They destroyed it."

The question's there, lingering in her gaze. "I'm well aware of that," she says, then swallows loud enough to hear. "Is it really about a debt for you?"

"Would I ask you to marry me if I only cared about a debt?" I question her unspoken thoughts.

Time pauses and it feels like I have her back, like she's close enough to hold on to forever so long as I don't slip up.

"The suggestion wasn't asked, it was told. In order to save me from having to testify… It's not the same."

When she speaks, she's careful with every word. "I don't want to be under your thumb, Jase," she admits. "That's all this is. I'm playing into your hands over and over. I think I have control in situations when I don't."

I'm just as careful with my reply. "I know I fucked up. I shouldn't have let you see me like that--"

"Why?" she cuts me off. "Why wait there for me to see? You had to know I would."

And just like that, she's slipping away again.

I can't fucking breathe. This damn shirt feels like a noose around my neck; I clutch at it, unbuttoning my collar.

"I need you right now." The words fall from me and I'm not even aware that they have until she threads her fingers between mine and squeezes.

"You can tell me," she whispers.

How do I tell her the truth: I killed a man who hurt a woman I barely knew and it doesn't feel like it was enough? How do I tell her I can't get what happened years ago out of my head and the sight from that night will never leave me? How do I share that burden with anyone?

Let alone with her, a woman I can't lose? I'm barely conscious of it myself.

"Jase, I deserve to know."

My gaze drifts from hers and finds Seth's in the rearview mirror.

"I don't have answers right now."

"That's becoming a theme for you, isn't it?" she bites back, pulling her warm hand away from mine. Leaning forward she places her hand on the leather seat in front of her. "Seth, please take me home."

There's no room for negotiation in my tone. "You're coming home with me."

"The hell I am--"

"You belong with me!" The scream tears from me before I can stop it. Chaos erupts from hating the blur of failure around me and the uncertainty.

I feel insane. The stress of everything that's happened is driving me mad and I'm losing the only person who can keep me grounded. I can't look her in the eyes, knowing how badly I've failed her but she makes me, her fingers brushing the underside of my jaw until my gaze lifts to hers.

"I didn't say that I wasn't still with you. I didn't say I don't belong to you." She pauses, halting her words and seemingly questioning her last statement.

I won't allow it. She can't question that. Above all else, she needs to believe with every fiber in her that she belongs to me.

My fingers splay through her hair as I kiss her. With authority and demanding she feel what I can't say. She meets every swift stroke of my tongue with her own demands.

Reveling in it, I remind her of what we have.

This won't come around again. I can feel it in my bones. What we have is something we can't let go of. I've never been surer of anything in my life as I am of this.

It takes her a moment to push me away, with both hands on my chest. It's a weak gesture, but I give it to her and love how breathless I've left her.

Barely breathing, she alternates her stare between my lips and my eyes before nipping my lower lip.

The small action makes me feel like everything will be okay. I'm all too aware that's exactly what it's intended to do.

"Come home with me." It's not a command; I'm practically begging her.

She doesn't say no, but she doesn't say yes either. "You scare me. *This*," she says and gestures between the two of us, "scares me."

"Do you think it doesn't scare me too? That fear doesn't have a grip on me sometimes?"

"I didn't ask for this," she answers and when she does, her voice cracks, the emotion seeping in.

"I didn't either, but I'm not afraid to make known what I want. I won't let fear do that to me."

"I'm not saying this isn't what I want. I'm saying I need to breathe for a minute. You need to take me home."

It's then that I realize the car has stopped at the fork that determines which way we'll go.

"Take me home." Bethany whispers the statement like it's a plea. Seth waits for my order and when I nod, the car goes right, heading toward her house.

"I'm giving you space, Bethany. But it's temporary."

She doesn't let me off so easily. "Are you willing to tell me whose blood was on my shirt?"

I shake my head, but offer her a question in its place. "Are you willing to seriously consider my offer?"

"Offer?" The fact that she's forgotten so easily hurts more than I'll ever admit.

"Marry me."

"Tell me what happened."

"Say yes." Neither of us budge, neither of us give anything more than the gentle touch of our fingers meeting on the leather seats.

"When I marry someone, it will be because I never want to be away from them. Not because I involved myself with someone who doesn't trust me, who keeps secrets from me. Someone I know I shouldn't be with and who's giving me every reason to run."

I can't come up with an answer. I have nothing. Words never fail me like this.

"Everyone's entitled to a moment. But if you're going to keep it to yourself, prepare to be by yourself."

All I can give her is a singular truth as the car slows to a stop in front of her house. "I won't be by myself for long, Bethany."

"You will if you don't figure out how to answer my questions, Jase. I'm not in the habit of helping those who don't want to help themselves."

CHAPTER 3

Bethany

The Coverless Book
Twentieth Chapter
Jake's perspective

"She's a healer. She'll help you get better."

"I'm fine, Jake," Emmy pleads with me. I know she's scared to be in the woods searching out a woman some call a witch, but I won't let her die.

Staring at the dried herbs that hang from a line outside the leather tent, Emmy hesitates. "It's nearly twice a week," I tell her and my fingers slip through hers. She's lost weight and she looks so much paler than she did nearly a month ago when we ran away.

"The farmer's sister is nice, they're all nice, but she's not helping you."

We've been staying in a small cabin on the back of a farm in exchange for labor. It would be perfect this way... if Emmy didn't get sick and spit up blood so often.

"Please. Do it for me."

Her eyes are what draw me to her. She can't hide a single thought or feeling. They all flicker and brighten within her gaze. Her lips part just slightly but before she can kiss me or I can kiss her, a feminine voice calls out to our right, "Are you ready?"

Emmy immediately grabs me and hides just behind my left side. She doesn't take her eyes from the woman though. Shrouded in a black cloak, it's harder to see her among the shrubbery, but as she unveils her hood and walks toward the fire, the light shows her to be nothing more than human.

"Jake..." *Emmy protests.*

"For me," *I remind her, squeezing her hand after prying it from my hip and following the woman under the various tanned hides that protect her potions and remedies.*

"I know what ails you, but tell me what you think, my dear?" *The healer doesn't look at me; she doesn't speak to me at all. Emmy's quiet, assessing at first, but quickly she speaks up.*

I only watch the two of them taking a place in the corner, quietly praying to whatever gods may be listening, to help Emmy. I can't lose her.

"When I'm with him, I'm invincible."

The healer's smile wanes as she places her hand just above Emmy's but quickly takes it away, snatching a bag of something dried... flowers maybe? "Take these," *she says as she hands the bag to Emmy.* "You like soup, don't you?" *The chill of the night spreads under the tent, the wind rustling everything inside.* "It'll take the pain away."

"When I'm with him, I'm invincible."

I keep dragging my eyes back to that underlined line. She's changed. Emmy's changed. When did she need Jake to be invincible? And more importantly, why did he let that happen?

I have to remind myself that it's fiction. With that thought, I put down the book and force myself to face my own reality. I'm sure as hell not invincible. Not with Jase Cross and not without him either.

Laura's never going to believe me.

It's funny how I keep thinking about telling her what happened as if it's the worst hurdle to overcome at this point.

Telling your friend you lost hundreds of thousands of dollars they loaned to you... or gave to you, whichever... the thought of telling her that makes me feel sick to my stomach.

I have to rub my eyes as I get up off the sofa, The Coverless Book sitting right in front of me, opened and waiting on the coffee table. I couldn't close my eyes last night without seeing Officer Walsh, the blood on the floor, or Jase's intense gaze and the demons beneath that darkness.

Rest didn't come for me last night, no matter how badly I prayed for it.

Beep, beep, beep. Gathering my mug of hot-for-the-third-time coffee, I promise myself I'll remember to drink it this time as I test the temperature and find it acceptable to drink.

The last time I burned the tip of my tongue.

My cell phone stares back at me. The book stares back at me. The door calls to me to go back to Jase.

And yet all I can do is sit back on my sofa, stretching in the worn groove and staring across the room at a photo of my sister in her high school graduation cap with her arm wrapped around a younger, happier version of me.

Life wasn't supposed to turn out this way.

She was never supposed to go down that path and leave me here all alone.

"I still hate you for leaving me," I speak into the empty room even though I don't believe my own words. "But damn do I miss you." Those words are different. Those I believe with everything in me.

I wish I could tell her about Jase and the shit I've gotten myself into.

If only I had my sister back.

There are multiple stages of grief. I had at least three courses that told me all the stages in detail. I had to take all three to work at the center. If you're going to work with patients who are struggling with loss, and a lot of our patients are, you have to know the stages inside and out.

Acceptance comes after depression. It's the final stage and I've heard people tell me that they can feel it when it happens.

I used to think it was like a weight off their shoulders, but a woman told me once it was more like the weight just shifted somewhere else. Somewhere deeper inside of you, in that place where the void will always be.

Denial.
Anger.
Bargaining.
Depression.
Acceptance.

The five stages in all their glory. I've read plenty about them and at the time I associated each one with how I felt when my mother died, but maybe every death is different. Because this feels nothing like what I felt with her.

There are so many reasons to explain the differences. But one thing I can't make sense of is how I feel, with complete certainty, that I've accepted Jenny's death too soon. A month since she's been missing, weeks since her death.

I'm not ready to accept I'll never see her again, but I have. How fair is that?

"Do you hate me for it?" I ask the smiling, teenage version of my sister, with her red cap in her hand. "Can you forgive me for accepting you're gone forever so soon?"

Wiping harshly under my eyes, I let the exasperated air leave me in a sharp exhale. "And now I'm going crazy, talking to no one." I swallow and sniff away the evidence of my slight breakdown before confessing. "Not the person you were in the end, but the real you. Could the real you forgive me?"

As if answering or interrupting me, or maybe hating my confession—I'm not sure which—the old floor creaks. It does that when the seasons change. When the weather moves from bitter cold to warm. The old wood stretches and creaks in the early mornings.

Still, I can't breathe for the longest time, feeling like someone's with me.

Any sense of safety has vanished.

I wish Jase were here. It's my first thought.

Even when he hides from me, I still wish he were here. I'm choosing to stay away and yet, I wish he were here. How ironic is that?

The back and forth is maddening. Be with him, simply because I want to. Or hold my ground because he can't give me what I've given him. Truth and honesty in their rawest form. He makes me feel lower than him, weaker and abandoned. It's hard to turn a blind eye to that simply because I want his protection and his touch.

It hurts more knowing I went through my darkest times naked in his bed. Bared to him, not hiding this weakness that took me over. He couldn't even tell me what happened that landed my pathetic ass in jail.

Without a second thought, I snatch my phone off the table and dial a number. Not the one I've been thinking about. It's not the conversation I've been having in my head and obsessing about for the last hour.

No. I'm calling someone to get my life back. My life. My rules. My decisions. My happiness.

The phone rings one more time in my ear before I hear a familiar voice.

"There's only one thing I've ever had control over in my entire life, and it's been taken away from me."

"Jesus Christ, Bethany. Could you be any more dramatic?" My boss sounds exasperated, annoyed even and that only pisses me off further.

Leaning forward on the couch, I settle my heels into the deep carpet and prepare to say and do anything necessary to get my job back.

"I need this, Aiden," I say and hate that my throat goes dry. "I can't sit around thinking about every little detail anymore."

"Did you take a vacation?" he asks me.

"No."

"You need to get out of town and relax." The way he says 'relax' feels like a slap in the face. Is that what people do when they're on leave for bereavement?

"I don't want to relax; I just want to get back to normalcy."

"You need to adapt and change. That takes a new perspective."

Adapt and change. It's what we tell our patients when they're struggling. When they no longer fit in with whatever life they had before. When they can't cope.

"Knock it off," I say, and my voice is hard. "I'm doing fine. Better than fine," I lie. It sounds like the truth though. "I need to feel like me, though. You know me, Aiden. You know work is my life."

"Go take a vacation and I'll think about it while you're soaking in the sun."

"I can't." I didn't realize how much I needed to go back to work until the feeling of loss settles into my chest like cement.

"Well, you can't come back."

"Why the hell not? Why can't I go back to what was?"

"Why can't things go back? Do you hear yourself, Bethany?"

"Stop it," I say and the request sounds like a plea. "I'm not your patient."

"Your leave is mandatory. You aren't welcome back until the leave is over."

"My patients are my life."

"That's the problem. They shouldn't be. You need something more."

"I don't want something more." The cement settles in

deeper, drying and climbing up to the back of my mouth. It keeps more lies from trickling out.

"I'm looking out for you. Go find it." The click at the other end of the line makes me fall back onto the sofa, not as angry as I wish I was.

Fuck Aiden. I'll be back at work soon. I just have to survive until then. I hope I remember this moment for those long nights when I can't wait for my shift to end.

Swallowing thickly, I consider what he said.

I need something else.

Something more.

A memory forms an answer to the question: what is my "something more?"

Marry me.

My palm feels sweaty as I grip the phone tighter, then let it fall to the cushion next to me.

Marry me. His voice says it differently in my head. Different from the memory where he told me to do so because then I wouldn't have to testify against him.

I can't see straight or think straight. I'm caught in the whirlwind that is Jase Cross.

Knock, knock, knock.

Startled by the first knock, feeling as if I've been spared by the second, I stop my thoughts in their track. Someone at the front door saves me from my hurried thoughts, but the moment I stand to go to the door, I hesitate.

I shouldn't be scared to answer the door. I shouldn't feel the claws of fear wrapping around my ankles and making me second-guess taking another step.

I will not live in fear. The singular thought propels me further, but it doesn't stop me from grabbing the baseball bat I put in the corner of the foyer last night. The smooth wood slips in my palm until I grip it tighter and then quietly peek through the peephole.

Thump. Thump.

My heart stops racing the second I let out a breath, then put the baseball bat back to unlock the door and pull it open. "What the fuck is wrong with me," I mutter to myself.

"Mrs. Walker," I say and then shut the door only an inch more as the harsh wind blows in. "I wasn't expecting you."

The older woman purses her thin lips in a way that lets me know she's uncomfortable. She has the same look every time she stands to speak at the HOA meetings. Which she's done every time I've been there. I glance behind her to check my lawn, but the grass hasn't even started to grow yet.

"Is there something I can help you with?"

Her hazel eyes reach past me, glancing inside my house and I close the door that much more until it's open just enough for my frame, and nothing more.

"Is your grandson doing all right?" I ask her, reminding her about the last time we spoke. When she needed help and I came to her aid. Technically to her grandson's aid, who'd been struggling with his parents' divorce and needed someone to talk to.

"I was wondering if you were all right?" she clips back.

"Me?"

"There's been some activity… some men around your house lately." Her eyes narrow at me, assessing and I'm not sure what she'll find. I close the door behind me to step outside on the porch.

"Men?" I question.

"A number of them. In cars that seem... expensive. Same with the clothes."

"Are you suggesting I'm some sort of escort, Mrs. Walker?" I throw in a bit more contempt than I should, in an attempt to get her to back off.

"No. I think they're drug dealers." Her answer isn't judgmental. Just matter of fact.

The tiny hairs on the back of my neck stand on end and I have to cross my arms a bit tighter.

"This is what happened to your sister. Isn't it?"

Words escape me. The memory of my sister on the steps right in front of me causes the cold to seep into my skin, and then deeper within. I can see her there still. I can't tear my eyes away from her. God help me, I'm losing it. She looks just as I saw her last. Except for her hair, she's wearing it like our mom used to. Memories flood my thoughts. None of them good.

"Are you all right? You're as white as the snow," Mrs. Walker says as she grips my shoulder and I snap, pulling myself away from her.

"Please leave me alone," I tell her and refuse to look back at my sister. I can feel Jenny's gaze on me. It's like she's sitting right there on the porch steps. Watching us now, but not saying anything.

I don't move until Mrs. Walker does, leaving in silence. It's only when she's walking down the stairs that I dare look at them.

My sister's not there. Of course she's not. She's gone. My sister's gone.

Whipping my door open, I pace in the hall.

What the fuck is wrong with me? I need to get the fuck out of here.

My keys jingle as I lift them from the hook in my foyer. I nearly leave just as I am: unshowered and in pajamas. I haven't even brushed my hair yet today. With my hand on the doorknob, I settle my nerves.

Just take one breath at a time. One day at a time.

Shower. Dress. And then I'm heading to Laura's.

She'll help me. She has to know a way out.

If Jase loves me, he'll give me space. I just need to breathe. He'll understand if I go away for just a little while. I'll do what Aiden said. I'll go away. Somewhere no one knows. I have to get away from here. Somewhere in the back of my mind, my inner bitch is laughing at me for thinking Jase would ever let me leave. He doesn't know what my mother told me though. I can't fall for him. I can't risk it and knowing that makes me want to run faster than I've ever run in my life.

Chapter 4

Jase

It's always quiet out here. Although it was quiet last time as well, and that's when everything fell apart.

Rows and rows of stones. Centuries have passed and nothing's changed. I think that's why I come here. It doesn't matter what happened before or after, the stones stay in familiar rows like silent sentinels.

I've lived with many regrets and many failures. It's not often that I can see them the moment they happen. I shouldn't have told her to marry me. Now that it's done though, I can't stop from wanting to tell her again and again until she agrees.

I can make that right.

Unlike so many other things I can't fix. The gust of breeze blows dried flower petals across the gravestone before me. With the petals clear of it, it's easy to read my brother's name etched in stone.

I'll make it right with her. There's only so much I can make right, and she deserves it. Not many do.

If I had to pinpoint a time when everything changed, a single moment when everything went wrong, I'd be forced to choose between two.

The first is the moment Romano hired a hit on me that went awry and resulted in a funeral for my closest brother. An old soul at such a young age, he never did anything to anyone. Tragedy changes a man forever.

If fate had ended its interference there, I don't think my brothers and I would have a normal life, but it wouldn't be one so cruel. Maybe one more empty though.

"I figured I'd find you here," Seth calls out from a distance. Shoving his hands into his black windbreaker he makes his way to me. I'm not ready to leave though.

The second moment is when Carter was taken by Nicholas Talvery, beaten, and changed into a broken boy hell-bent on fighting the men who lived to destroy us. He blazed the path for us, viciously and mercilessly. Because of him we stayed. We didn't have to run; we were more than capable of fighting together.

Two old men, men who ruled ruthlessly, they're the ones so easy to blame.

Since then, everyone has left us and no one could be trusted. Pillars of life crumbled to insignificant dust in favor of simply surviving and adapting to be more like them. To dedicate our lives to destroying them before they could do the same to us.

I hate what we've become, but I can't let go of how it all started and what still needs to be done.

Talvery is dead; Romano is close to gone, but Marcus

is still here. Still giving orders, still deciding everyone's fate as if it's his right. They may be the root cause of it all, but Marcus planted the seeds, Marcus knew.

"I'll make them all pay." The promise to my brother drifts away in the bitter wind.

"What's that?" Seth asks and then braces against the harsh chill, zipping his jacket before glancing at the stone on the ground. I can see the question written on his face, but he doesn't voice it. Instead he tells me, "I didn't hear what you said."

He's taller than me, just barely. But on the hill of the grave he looks taller still.

"You found me," I comment and huff a sarcastic laugh. "Should have gone somewhere else."

"I have good news and bad. I didn't think you'd want to wait for either," Seth tells me, and the way he lowers his voice suggests an apologetic tone.

"Let's have the good news first," I tell him, staring off into the distance past the rows of gravestones to the green grass, waiting to be filled.

"There are patterns in the movements of the men we've been watching." Seth takes a half step closer and adds, "Marcus's men."

I focus all my attention back to Seth. "Patterns?" He nods and says, "Between the ferry and the trains. They're transporting something."

The smell of fresh dirt and sod blow by us as he adds, "They're spending a lot of time at each location. Declan thinks there are holding points."

"And what about Marcus? Where is he?"

"We don't know yet."

"Find him." My answer is clipped, but easy enough. It's progress in this slow game of chess and we're carefully moving pieces on the board.

"Bethany still doesn't know about Jenny?"

"No. I'm not telling her until I know where she is and that she's alive still."

"Right," he says. The single word brings defeat to the air and I can't place my finger as to why. "I don't know that we'd be able to sneak up on him or set something up without him knowing. He has eyes everywhere. The more people we follow, the more are involved--"

I cut him off, knowing the risk involved, knowing Marcus will more than likely know when we come for him. "Just find him."

"Of course. I'm on it."

"And the bad news?"

CHAPTER 5

Bethany

"Why don't we take it from the top?" Laura asks me in her living room as I pace in front of the floor-to-ceiling windows that look out over the park. Although, from up here on the twentieth floor, it's merely a square of green.

"Which top?" I ask her. "The one that involves Jase or the one that's easier to swallow?"

"I get the easy one, you're on leave and need to go on vacation before Aiden will quit being an ass. That one I've got. How about the one where you went to jail?"

"I don't think I was technically in jail since I never saw a cell." I don't stop my pacing.

"So the money is gone, but Jase doesn't care. All the evidence is gone and he wants you to marry him just in case this happens again?"

I only nod.

"See, it's the marriage thing that I may be hung up on..." she trails off as she lowers herself to a dusty rose velvet chair and takes a sip from her tall wine glass. She settled on prosecco when I said I didn't want any coffee and word-vomited up everything—including seeing my sister on my front porch steps. I'm surprised she didn't go straight for the vodka.

"The 'marry me' part? Not seeing my dead sister and feeling her there?"

She shrugs. "Sometimes we see what we want to see. You feel alone and need someone to talk to. You didn't want to tell me about the money. She was your rock for a long time..."

Was. Past tense. My steps slow to a stop as I pull my still-damp-from-the-shower hair away from my face and look back down at the park.

"I'm sorry about the money," I say and have to clear my throat after speaking. I'd say anything for her not to bring up Jenny again. She's gone. Truly gone.

Fuck. It shouldn't hurt like this still, should it?

"Don't worry about the money--"

Cutting her off, I ask, "Will you hide me?" Shock flashes in her eyes. Swallowing thickly, I continue, "I don't know how you got the money, but there's obviously a lot I don't know. If there's any way to hide me—please do it. I just need to get away for a while."

"Away from Jase, you mean?" She barely says the words and I nod.

"I need to cope and think on my own and he's just..."

"All consuming," she finishes my statement for me, but

somehow the words seem to be meant for someone else as she looks past me, staring at the white and blush striped curtains instead.

"Yes."

She nods once, downing her glass and then standing up, all the while not looking at me. As she rounds the corner to her kitchen, no doubt to fill her glass, she tells me, "I have someone I can call. I can ask him for a favor."

Hope is nowhere in her cadence; her tone is resigned.

I can feel some hope though. A tiny bit at the idea of being away for just a little while. Enough to get out of the chaos. Enough to breathe. Taking out my phone, I contemplate telling Jase just that. To give me space and time. That I'll be back.

I slip my phone back into my jeans. Not yet. He's not going to like it. He needs to get over it, though. There are plenty of things I don't like about this arrangement either, and I've rolled with the punches as best as I can. I return to gazing at the park and brush my fingers against the cool glass. I've never felt like this before. I've never been so… so helpless.

I hear Laura before I see her and I'm quick to turn my back on my reflection as she lets out a long breath.

"Did you call?" I ask her and she doesn't answer immediately. Instead she stares through me, looking to the park outside.

She snaps out of it as I bite out her name.

"What?"

"Did you call?" I ask her again and an eerie feeling crawls over my skin at the way she swallows before answering me, although she only nods.

"What's wrong?" I question her and she shakes her head, then returns to her seat.

"It's just work. Not you."

Relief isn't so forthcoming, but I don't think Laura's lying to me. Especially not when she offers me a tight smile.

"Is it Michelle? Is she okay? I heard dealing with the pica condition has been difficult."

Her hair swishes as she shakes her head. "She's doing fine. All your patients are fine," she says as she leans back, moving her hair to one side and braiding it. "Don't worry about them, you workaholic, you."

"What is it then?" I ask her. "Anything I can do to help?"

"Did I tell you about the patient with no name?" she says and her features turn serious. A haunting memory reveals itself in her eyes.

"Just initials?"

"Right. The woman with only initials…" She pauses before telling me the rest. "Somehow… someway, she got hold of a bottle of antifreeze."

"What the hell?"

"She tried to kill herself. She drank the entire thing and needed an emergency transfusion. Every ounce of her blood had to be drained for her not to die."

"How could that have even happened? That's impossible." She shakes her head only ever so slightly, but her expression holds a different answer. My hands tremble as I walk toward her. I can't believe it. "When did this happen?"

"Three days ago."

"How the hell did it happen?" I walk closer to her, unable to contain the horror and shock that a patient in our facility was able to obtain a means to end it.

"That's the thing," she says and looks me dead in the eyes. "There is no investigation."

Chills flow down my arms. All my concerns seem so meaningless in comparison. I've never been so grateful for a tragedy.

"She had to have dialysis, the antifreeze did so much damage. We were waiting to hear what kind of inquiries would be made. What paperwork and interviews we needed to prepare for… but Aiden told us that it never happened. To act like there was no incident and not to speak a word of it. So you… you better not tell him I told you."

"How can there be no investigation?" The question leaves me slowly, barely able to form itself.

"Whoever is paying for her to be there paid for the antidote, the dialysis… all of it with cash and they don't want any attention brought to it."

I drop into the seat next to her, processing it all and unable to shake the cold sensation that's taken over.

"Whoever it is, they want her there and they don't want anyone to know about it."

"Did they give her the antifreeze?" I dare to question.

"No. Aiden's the only one on her charts. After he told us, I followed him to his office." She swallows thickly. "I think it was an accident. He's on her charts, bringing her items she asked for. I think he made a mistake. But I don't understand why he's not fired. He should have checked it."

"Aiden? No." I can't believe that. Aiden's better at his job than that.

"I think he fucked up. She's smart and wants to die. Really wants to die." She licks her lower lip and then tells me, "But whoever's paying for all of this? They want her alive."

A cheerful series of dings in different octaves fills the room, forcing her knuckles to turn white as she grips the chair and then cusses beneath her breath.

"Your doorbell is going to give you a heart attack," I comment and then look to the large cobalt door. "Who is that?"

She doesn't look back at me as she stands and tells me, "The person I called."

There are little moments when you know someone's screwed you over before they show their cards.

It's in the way they talk; the way they look at you. Even the way Laura walks right now. Unlocking the deadbolt and opening the door without speaking, without checking to see who it is.

All the while I sit there, denying this feeling of betrayal as if it's not really happening.

Even when Seth walks through the door, tall, handsome and demanding Seth, I still want to deny it.

"I'm tired of being the last to know," is all I can mutter, leaning back and hating that the last person I had in my corner denied me a chance to get out of this mess. "I suppose it's my problem to deal with, isn't it?"

I can hear her apologies, her pleas for me to understand all the while Seth is saying something, but it's all white noise. I'm not interested in hearing what her excuse is. She of all people should know I need to get away. She lives in solace. She preaches it to me constantly.

"So, Seth?" I finally speak up although my ass is still firm in the chair. "Seth's who you called? Or did you go straight to Jase?"

They both speak at the same time.

"You have to forgive me, Bethany—I didn't have a choice."

"Jase doesn't have to know you were thinking about leaving him."

The chair pushes back against the wall; it would have tipped over if the wall hadn't been there to block its path because I stood so quickly.

"First off, you always have a choice," I push the words through clenched teeth at Laura and then turn to Seth. "Secondly, I wasn't leaving him. I wasn't running, so fucking tell him for all I care!" I don't mean to scream.

I don't mean to lose control. *Who the fuck am I kidding? What control did I ever have?*

"Beth, please," Laura says as she reaches out for me and I snatch my arm away.

"How could you?" I can't look at her. Not because of anger. Because of the hurt that rests across my chest.

"One day I'll tell you why. Just forgive me," she pleads with me.

"I love you," I tell her. "But right now, I really hate you."

She covers her mouth with one hand and watches me walk to Seth, who hasn't moved from the threshold.

"Seth."

"Bethany." He says my name sweeter than I say his. He even affords me a smile. "Are you ready?"

"No. No, I'm not. I wasn't expecting you. When I asked my *good* friend," I pause to look at her from the corner of my eyes, only to see her leaning against the wall. Her arms are crossed over her chest and her focus is straight ahead at the window rather than at us. "When I asked her to call someone, I wanted to leave. Not go back to Jase." Before he can respond I add, "Not right now. I just need to breathe."

"No, you don't," he tells me as if he knows what I need. As if he knows what I'm going through.

"I hear things. I see things. I don't feel okay." I don't expect my voice to crack or the admission to stir up so much emotion, but it does.

"Hey," he says then reaches out to brush my shoulder, and I notice how that gets Laura's attention, how she watches him touch me.

He squeezes my shoulder gently when he tells me, "It's going to be all right." His voice is soothing, his dark eyes calming. "Come on, come with me." Seth holds out his hand for me to take once he's released his grip, as if he's some sort of savior. "Jase doesn't know, but you should tell him what you're feeling."

Guilt isn't something I expected to feel.

"If she wants to, she will." Laura speaks up for me, and when I look back at her over my shoulder, I can see her swallow and it's not until I nod that she nods too.

I already forgive the two-timing bitch. I don't understand, though. I'll never understand why she sold me out.

Seth's eyes stay on Laura's a moment longer as he speaks, right before he looks back down to me, letting his hand fall to his side. "He's going through something right now. He's making mistakes and focusing all his time and energy on you. It's causing problems."

"He shouldn't." I refuse to be used as an excuse for someone else.

"I know that. He knows that too."

He starts to say something else but I cut him off. "I'll drive home myself."

"I wanted to show you something."

"I don't want to see anything, talk about anything, or do anything at all but have a moment to just be away from all of this," I practically hiss. "What can't you understand about that?" Anger and desperation twine together. "I'm not okay, but I'm trying to be."

"I wanted to show you something. But it can wait. We have time. Plenty of time. If you want to go home, know that I have to keep an eye on you."

"How's it feel to be a babysitter?" I can't help the snide comment although I immediately apologize. "I'm not usually such a bitch," I comment after he accepts.

"You could tell me whatever it is. I could go there myself."

He only shakes his head.

"If you could be a non-problem… he has enough of them."

"Wouldn't me leaving be exactly that?" I already know the answer before it's fully spoken.

"The fuck it is." His quick response and even scorn at the thought throw me off. "He needs you by his side." His statement strikes me at my core. The emotional crack destroys what little resolve I have left.

"I just don't know if I'm the woman that can be by his side." I almost tell him I don't know if I can be by anyone's side. Especially not now, with every day passing and the warning my mother gave me sounding louder and louder in my mind.

"Well, he chose you. And between the two of us, I know you are."

CHAPTER 6

Jase

"HOW COULD YOU BE SO FUCKING RECKLESS?"

I don't answer my brother. The silence is deafening as my shoulders tense and I lean against his desk with both my fists planted on the edge of it. He refused to wait for this meeting and demanded it happen right now; that's how I knew he was aware of my fuckup.

Neither of us say anything. I can feel his eyes on me as he turns from the windows in his office and slowly takes his seat. The smell of polished leather and old books invades my senses as I do the same, sitting across from him and feeling the disappointment flow through me.

The need to check on Bethany rides me hard as I sit there. All I can think about is Bethany and how I hurt her.

Seth's watching her though. *She's fine.* I've been telling

myself that repeatedly since I left her. That, and that she'll forgive me. That she just needs space.

She loves me. I remember that she told me she did once. The reminder doesn't feel so truthful anymore.

"It's unacceptable." I say the words so he doesn't have to. "What I did could have cost us everything." All I can think about is Bethany, and all he can think about is the mistake I made. The first one in a long damn time.

"The fucking FBI is breathing down our necks and you do that?" Carter doesn't hide the rage as he slams his fist down.

I don't react. This is how he is and how I knew he'd be. He can scream all he wants. What's done is done and his display of anger won't change that.

I don't say anything for the longest time, until finally, "I know," is somehow spoken from my lips.

"What the fuck were you thinking, leaving like that? You drove in public while covered in blood. It would have taken a single phone call. We don't flaunt this shit. It's one fucking rule none of us has ever broken." His chaotic breathing has lessened. The cords in his neck are no longer as tense.

In this moment, he reminds me so much of our father. Maybe because he's focusing his rage at me for the first time that I can ever remember. "Everything we do is with reason and intention. Careful. Meticulous. We don't leave evidence." Every word is spoken calmer and more relaxed. He even sits back in his seat before running a hand down his face.

"What were you thinking?" he asks again.

"I don't know."

My answer is quick, as is his rebuttal. "Bullshit."

"Bull-fucking-shit," he repeats and with his words, the sky darkens behind him. The night is settling in, as is his disbelief. My knuckles rap in synchrony on the wooden armrests of my chair as he looks at me, and I look at him.

"You always know what you're doing. You're always in control, yet you did it anyway." His voice is calm, his composure returned. Tilting his chin up, he asks me, "Why? You had to have known she'd see and that you were risking everyone else seeing just so she could see."

"I shouldn't have-"

"But you did. You wanted her to see you, Jase. There's no other explanation. You don't fuck up like this. None of us fuck up like this."

My brother's words hang heavy in the air. Waiting for me to accept them.

"She doesn't need to see what I do. What I'm capable of."

"You wanted her to, though."

"I won't do it again," is all I answer him, still not wanting to accept I'd do something so stupid and reckless. "I was emotional. I was caught up in the past."

"You wanted her to see," he repeats and I lift my gaze to his dark eyes.

"It doesn't matter. It'll never happen again."

He looks like he wants to say something else. Like the words are just there, right on the tip of his tongue, toying with the idea of falling off.

The room is silent though. For a moment and then another.

"She doesn't need to see that," I tell him, content with

that truth and then I crack my knuckles one at a time. "I won't do it again."

"She already knew, Jase." I pin my gaze to my brother's. "Even if she doesn't admit it. She already knew."

"Knew what?"

"What you were capable of. She knows what you do. She already knows. You're right that you don't need to show her. But you're wrong to think she didn't already know."

With an open palm, my hand moves to the harsh stubble surrounding my mouth and then to my jaw.

"Some part of you wanted to know what she really thought of it all. Is that it?"

I ignore his question. "I scared her."

"She should fear what you're capable of. It's new to her." Carter leans forward on his desk, resting his elbows on the hard wood and it gets my attention as what he says registers.

"What do I do now?"

A flicker of a grin shows on Carter's face. "Because I should know what to do when the woman I love fears me?"

"I didn't say that."

"What are you saying then?"

"I'm saying I fucked up, she's scared, and I don't want her to run." My voice lowers of its own accord and a confession escapes as I say, "I can't let her run." With my head lowering, I think back to the way she looked at me before closing her front door. She looked back at me the way she did in the restaurant. Like it may be the last time.

"She's not the only one afraid then, is she?"

"I'm asking for advice, Carter. It's not something I care to do often," I comment, hating the way something in my chest twists with agony.

"She's not like us; she didn't grow up in this world."

"She fixes the ones we break though. Addiction and loss... she stares that in the face every day."

"You think because she works at the Rockford Center that she could handle seeing you covered in blood?"

"I wasn't covered in it," I say. My rebuttal is useless.

"Not to her. She doesn't see *this*. This is different. It's not something she can control with a bed, pills and a conversation."

"Neither is loss. Loss isn't controlled." The need to defend her overrides my sensibility.

Carter's gaze is assessing. Running my hands through my hair, I question my own sanity.

"She's under your skin." Carter's tone verges on discouragement.

"Which is right where I want her to be," I admit freely, correcting him. "I'm not letting her go."

"Then don't allow her to see what frightens her without first giving her a way to handle it. You blinded her to what's going on, then showed Bethany her own worst fears without warning. What did you think would happen?"

"I wasn't thinking," I mutter, staring at the dark red in the carpet beneath our feet.

"Start using your head again. How's that for advice?"

It's hard to hold back from rolling my eyes. "Any other advice you want to offer?"

"Promise her she doesn't have to be a part of this world if she doesn't want to. You should have never come back like that... She's seen already, she knows and she hasn't walked away."

"What if I can't hide it all from her? What if I don't want to hide it?" The truth is buried in the questions, something that loosens the tension. Something that makes me feel like I can breathe again.

"She knew before, Jase," he repeats himself again. "You're fooling yourself if you think she didn't know who you were and the world you inhabit before."

"Knowing isn't the same as seeing," I comment and regret what I did. I regret losing it and putting her in a place to be shocked and frightened. "I'll do better." I make the promise to her, although Carter's the one who hears it and the one who gives a single nod.

"Do you know how I knew I should fight for Aria, rather than let her go?" Carter asks me and I wait for his answer. "Without her, I just can't go back to being without her. There is no version of my life where I'd be okay knowing she wasn't with me and not knowing if she was okay. I needed to make sure she was loved. I couldn't move forward not knowing if she would be loved if I weren't there."

There's that word again... *love*.

"If you want her, make her see that. She knew what she was getting into. She'll be exposed to more of our world over time and she'll learn to deal with it in a way she can. She didn't run, though. She's not going to leave you, Jase."

"Is that why you called me in here?" I ask him, watching the wind blow the trees in the distance behind him. "To give me advice and watch me sit here with my tail between my legs?"

The leather groans as Carter sits deeper in the wingback chair. "Romano's been indicted."

"Indicted?"

"The FBI agents that have set up camp aren't going to be leaving anytime soon. They're fucking everywhere."

"Did they find the explosives on the east side?"

"No, we got there first. Any evidence of an association with him has been wiped. But they're digging. So we need to be careful." I don't miss the way Carter looks at me when he says the word *careful*.

"You think he'll pay them off?" I ask.

"I think he'll try. I would."

His phone vibrates on the desk, halting the conversation momentarily. With a glance he sits up, and messages back. It must be Aria. "I've got to go; do you have anything else?"

"I want her to marry me." I say the words out loud. Freeing them. He's the one who brought up love. I've never considered him helping me, but he has Aria and if he can have her, I should be allowed to have Bethany.

"Then tell her." Carter's response is easy enough.

"I did."

"Was that before or after she was arrested?" I look past him, letting out a frustrated sigh. "You've never waited for anything. Why would a marriage proposal be any different?"

"Timing may not have been the best."

"Best?" Carter actually laughs. He has the balls to let out a deep, rough chuckle that fills the room and forces me to crack a smile.

"I told her she wouldn't be able to testify if we were married."

"You're a fucking dumbass, Jase. I'm a goddamn bull in a china shop and even I'm more graceful than that."

"It felt right." I drag my hand down my face remembering how her eyes widened.

"Like I said, you're a dumbass. You like shocking her," my brother comments. "I'm not sure that's exactly what she wants or needs from you at the moment."

"What does she want?" I say out loud and Carter answers as if he's known Beth her entire life.

"Someone to help her with the things that matter most to her. Someone to love her."

His phone vibrates again and that's when I check mine and my stomach drops. "She needs someone to kick her ass. That's what she needs," I murmur under my breath.

CHAPTER 7

Bethany

"SETH TOLD ME."

The heat in Jase's car is stifling. For the first time, he's driving and Seth is nowhere to be seen. It's just us.

"What did he tell you?" I ask.

"You said you wouldn't run," he says and his tone is accusatory.

A small and insignificant sigh falls from my lips as I stare at the passing trees, small buds forming on the branches and lean my head against the passenger side window. "I wasn't running."

The steady clicking of the blinker is the only sound until we turn at the end of the street. "What would you call it?" he asks me and I answer.

"Following my boss's orders to take a vacation while getting away from the chaos for a moment."

"You really think you would have come back?" I can tell from the huff that leaves him that he doesn't believe I would have.

"I would have missed you, worried about you and thought about you every second I was gone. You're a fool to think otherwise." I second-guess my harsh manner and turn to look at him. He only gives me his profile; he's still staring at the road. His stubble is longer than it's ever been, but I love the masculinity of it, along with his dominating features. "I'm sorry. I shouldn't have called you that."

Quiet. It's quiet and that's how I know he doesn't believe me. I suppose it works both ways. The mistrust between us runs deep with not just everything that's happened, but the way we've handled it all.

Laying a hand between us, palm up, I offer a truce. "I thought you'd come last night. I was waiting for you."

"You didn't message me."

"Neither did you." I give him back the same accusatory tone.

"Seth suggested that I give you space. Carter agreed with him. I thought I could use some as well, given that you made plans to leave."

"You scared me--"

"I apologized." His words cut me off and I steady myself, pulling my hand back to my lap.

"Do you want me to apologize? I'm sorry. I'm sorry I made you think I'd run." Transparency is what I'm aiming for, so I let the words spill out. Every bit honest. "I could've handled it differently. I didn't trust you'd let me go."

"You're damn right, I wouldn't have and I won't now."

Anger simmers inside of me until vulnerability stretches his next words. "You knew before."

My heart does a silly thing. It beats out of rhythm, making sure I'm listening to it. "Knew what?"

"You knew who I was."

"I still know. I'm still here, aren't I?"

He finally glances at me as the expensive car drives over gravel for a short moment, jostling the smooth ride.

"I would do anything for you. Name it, I'll do it. Whatever you need to make you want to stay."

"What?" I say and the word is as exasperated as I am. "What are you talking about?"

"If you want to leave, you come straight to me. In exchange," he says as he taps his thumb rapidly on the leather steering wheel. "Name it. Whatever you need in exchange for *me* being the person you run to."

I don't hesitate to take away the card he's been playing to keep me under his thumb as I say, "Drop the debt."

"It's dropped."

He says it too easily, too quickly. The words were waiting to be spoken. It didn't matter what I said. The long drive is winding as we approach the Cross estate. The dent in the fence is already fixed, but my mind replays the images of when I sped away as we drive by it.

"I don't believe you. The moment I do something you don't like or the second I make you think I'm leaving you, you'll say I owe you."

"I'll write it down in fucking blood, Bethany." There's no menace in his words, only desperation and he adds, "I'm trying," while staring into my eyes. I can feel it deep inside of me, his need to hold me.

I barely whisper, "Why do you want me?"

"Because you make it okay. You make it all right."

"I don't know what I'm making okay, Jase. Can't you understand how *that's* my problem?"

The car comes to a halt on the paved driveway and he lets out a long exhale, staring at the bricked exterior rather than at me before he tells me again, "I'm trying."

"I'll try too," I answer quickly, remembering the tit for tat our relationship started as and may always be. "Let's go back to the beginning. There's no debt this time, but I still have questions. I don't want to forget what happened to my sister. I want to know who. I want to know why."

Jase merely stares at his front door as he turns off the car. Not speaking, not acknowledging what I've said for so long that I eventually move closer to him and almost repeat my suggestions until he takes my hand in his and squeezes lightly.

Hope moves between us, drawing us closer.

"Can you give me a name?" I ask him, praying he'll trust me this time. It's a futile prayer.

"I'd rather not."

"Do you have anything new?"

"No."

I have to swallow to keep from telling him that there's no point if all he'll ever be is a sea of dark secrets to me. I nearly breathe out, *what's the point?* and storm off. I can already hear the car door slamming. Instead, I stay in the parked car with him, letting him hold my hand.

Our relationship is uneven; it may always be. Jase needs this. I think he needs it more than I do.

That's the point. This is for him. I can take what's mine

another time. "I don't know that I can live with all the secrets," I admit quietly.

"Ask me something else," Jase says, the slow stroke of his rough thumb pausing on my knuckles as the crisp chill enters the car in place of the heat.

"Whose blood was it?" I dare to ask. There's a pitter-patter in my chest that keeps me from inhaling when he hesitates.

Clearing his throat, he answers, "A man's. Someone who hurt a lot of people."

I push for more, staring at him, willing him to look at me, but he still doesn't.

"Name," I demand. "I deserve to know whose blood was on me."

"Hal."

Settling back into my seat, I note that he doesn't give me more, but he's given me something. "I don't think I like that name anymore."

My off-handed comment is rewarded with a slight huff of a laugh from Jase before he looks at me, really looks at me. The kind of look I'll remember forever. Not at all like the way he was in the bathroom this past weekend.

"Are you okay?" he asks me, and I don't know what prompted it.

"You really do scare me... sometimes."

"I don't want to."

I squeeze his hand when he stops squeezing mine and say, "I know you don't."

"Ask me something else," he says, looking out of the window.

"Are you okay?" It's all I can think to ask.

He nods once but doesn't say anything else and I get the feeling he's keeping something from me. Enough so that I open the car door and head inside. It takes a moment for him to follow. The wind is unkind, ushering us inside as quickly as possible.

It seems like this is temporary. That we're pretending it's okay when it's not. There's something unsettling in the air between us as we walk to the bedroom quietly, our steps even and echoing in the empty hall.

"Do you have a 'something?'" I ask him as his hand grips the doorknob. He twists and pulls it before looking down at me questioningly. "Something other than work?" I ask him and his answer strikes me hard. "Family. I have my brothers."

The pain of loss is a horrid thing. It comes and goes; it sneaks up on you but it also punches you in the face at times.

It feels like it's done all of those things to me in this moment. All at once.

Leaving Jase standing in the doorway, I drop my purse on the bed while kicking my shoes off without looking at him and try not to let it eat at me, but it is. Obviously so. Jase's keys clink on the dresser, then his watch before he takes off his jacket.

"I shouldn't have said that," he admits with his back to me before facing me. "I wasn't thinking."

The comfort of regret is what lifts my eyes to his.

"Yes, you should have. It's what I needed to hear."

Maybe he's my something.

There's no other logical explanation for why I'm so drawn to him. He's talking as he walks to me, saying something but I don't hear a word. Just the soothing cadence of his voice as I stare at his lips, his broad chest.

Just love me.

Pushing myself off the bed, I press my body to his, surprising him as I kiss him. It's needy, it's raw. His response is just as primitive. He tears the clothes from my body, but I don't move to remove his; I don't trust myself to loosen my hold on him. My fingers are braced at the back of his neck, keeping his lips to mine and urging him to devour me. To take from me, to use me. To make me feel alive and worthy of life.

I love you. The words are trapped inside of me. Maybe he can feel them when I kiss him. Maybe his lungs are filled with the knowledge when he breaks our kiss for only a moment to suck in air before tossing me onto the bed and then covering my body with his.

His fingers press on my inner thigh as his tongue delves into my mouth. Each stroke against my clit is sensual but demanding, just as Jase is. Every second I feel hotter. And with his palm pressing against my most sensitive area, a sweat breaks out along my skin so suddenly, I moan into the air and throw my head back to breathe.

He rocks his palm against my heat, and presses his hardened cock into my thigh. His stubble scratches along my neck and the sensation pushes me closer and closer until the all-consuming need throws me off the edge of my release.

"Spread your legs wider," he commands, pulling my thighs farther apart and I obey.

Breathless still with the waves of pleasure rocking through me, my nails dig into the bedsheets as I wait for him to settle between my hips.

There isn't an ounce of hesitation at having him between my legs after touching me like that.

The warmth of the high is still wrapped around me, making the small touches he gives me trace pleasure on my skin. "Are you expecting your period?" His question quickly changes that.

My lungs lurch and I'm quick to push him off of me.

"Fuck." Embarrassment rages in my heated cheeks and I climb off the bed as I snag my clothes, keeping my legs closed tight.

I can't look at him as I scatter to the bathroom, flicking on the light and digging through the basket in the cabinet under the sink. *Damn it. Damn it, damn it, damn it.*

I haven't had many sexual partners and it's been years since I've had a boyfriend, but the last time something like this happened, I stained the sofa cushion of my high school fling. The hollowness that comes with a dry throat and embarrassing memories takes over as I find a thin liner that will have to do for this moment.

I'm sitting there taking care of it all, feeling foolish and wondering if my period is why I've been so emotional and tired and down and unable to think right.

"Are you all right?" Jase's voice comes from outside the bathroom and I prepare to face him.

Opening the door to see him standing there, a small trail of hair leading down and drawing my eyes to the edge of the boxer briefs he slipped on, makes me that much more self-conscious. "I'm sorry."

"It's fine." His expression is easy, but the way he bites the edge of his lip and lets his gaze linger makes me feel anything but. "It's good you got it. We've been reckless."

I hesitate to respond when I look over his shoulder and see he's changed the sheets.

"Thank you for..." Closing my eyes and swallowing tightly, I fail to say the rest out loud.

"It's fine. Do you need anything?"

He leans against the doorjamb, not taking his eyes off of me. When he crosses his arms, his muscles become taut and I find myself feeling hot all over again.

I need my something. I need it more than anything.

A hint of worry crosses his expression when I don't answer him.

"I don't want to lose what we're building, Bethany. I don't want to lose you."

"Then don't."

Jase

I couldn't give two shits about her period.

I couldn't give two shits about her wanting to leave yesterday.

All I care about right now is pressing my body against hers, ravaging her, hearing those soft sounds slip from her lips. I'm still hard for her, still needing to feel her, to remind her how good it is.

"Strip down... all the way." With the simple command she stares up at me, her chest rising and falling heavily. Her hair is a messy halo and her hazel eyes are in disarray.

Leaning forward and bending down enough to whisper at the shell of her ear I say, "Don't make me tell you twice, my fiery girl."

Her eyes close and her head falls back instinctively. Like the good girl she is, her hands move to the button on her pants just as I unhook her bra through her shirt.

"You make me weak," she whispers.

"You do the same to me." No confession has ever felt so sinful to be spoken.

"You want to know why I want you?" I ask her, watching her undress and then stepping out of my boxer briefs to stroke my cock. "I can't get those little sounds you make out of my mind. They're addictive."

Her pale skin turns a bright red, flushing from her chest up to the temples of her hairline.

"You're beautiful, you're innocent in ways I find challenging, and a fighter in ways I respect." I've never thought about it like this before. I've never considered the specifics, and the statement forms itself as I take her nipple between my fingers and pull gently to direct her to the shower.

With a twist of the faucet and then the splash of hot water, steam billows toward us.

"You want to know why I want you?" she questions me as I grip her ass, one cheek in each hand and pull her up to me before stepping into the shower with her.

She gasps from the contrast of the hot water and the cold tile as I press her against the wall, but still keep us under the stream.

The warm water flows over my skin and it feels like heaven. Being cleansed and still having her in my grasp must be what heaven is like.

"Why?" I groan the word in the crook of her neck and then let my teeth drag down her skin, just to feel her squirm.

"Because you make me feel alive. You make me feel like everything matters and yet, nothing but you does."

I have to pull away to look down at her. Her hair's darker and wet, slick against her flushed skin.

Looking up at me through her thick lashes, I bring my lips just millimeters from hers and tell her, "You're damn right, nothing but us matters." Then I slam myself inside of her, letting her scream in pleasure in the hot stream. Her nails dig into my skin as I thrust inside of her, loving the feel of her tightening around my cock as she gets closer and closer.

Steadying her in my grasp, I keep my pace ruthless and deep as she bites into my shoulder to muffle her screams. I'd admonish her, forcing her to let me hear all the sweet noises she makes, but the hint of pain makes the pleasure that much more intense.

So I fuck her harder, silently begging her to bring me more of both the pleasure and the pain.

CHAPTER 8

Bethany

"ANYTHING YOU WANT, IS YOURS."

"You make big promises," I tell Jase as I follow him down the end of the hall. He keeps calling it a "wing" though. He says it's his wing of the estate.

Makeup sex is a real thing. There must be something special that happens to your brain when you have makeup sex. I'm convinced of it. I bet a decade of research could prove a thing or two to support that thought.

The kind of makeup sex that leaves you sore the day after. The kind of sore I am now.

"Anything within reason. Does that make you feel better?" he asks with a grin growing on his face. I can't help but to reach up and brush my thumb against his jaw.

He tells me lowly, "I need to shave," before I can sneak a small kiss that makes me rise up onto my tiptoes. A deep groan of satisfaction comes from his chest when I kiss him again.

"I like the stubble," I comment softly as we stop at the entrance to what looks like a library, one that's worthy of a museum. The antique weapons housed on a bookshelf full of creased leather spines and unique coverings draw me in.

Wow doesn't do it justice.

"The fireplace is real. It's from a castle in Ireland," he says as he walks to it on the other side of the room while my fingers trail down a set of old books with red covers. "Not like the glass one in the other room."

"Fireplaces seem to be your thing," I speak without really thinking about the words as my gaze drifts from one shelf to the next. "You like to read?" He nods. "And collect weapons?" I tilt my head at the knives on display. The bottoms of the blades have rust that extends to the handles.

"Yes," he answers and reaches out to gently caress my hip as I lean against him. The more I touch him, the more he touches me. Tit for tat, like all things with us.

"Where's your desk?" I ask, noting how it looks like a combination of a sitting room and office. "There should be a desk in here." The room has a primitive air to it, dark and cavernous with a large rug on the floor and walls covered with shelves.

"My office is at the bar. Not here. This is just for me." I lift my fingers from the books at his last comment until he adds, "And you, if you like it. You can come in here whenever you'd like."

I can imagine listening to the crackles of the fire as I turn the pages of The Coverless Book. "I think I'd enjoy that."

"Good, let me show you the rest."

Today is apparently the day Jase forces me to go on a tour. Between the gym, the cigar room and the billiard room, all three of which look entirely unused and are outfitted with as much dark polished wood as they are wealth, I'm not sure what Jase does as a hobby.

The only room he truly seems to enjoy is the office that's not an office... and the fire room. Which I've already explored with him.

"I love that you call it a fire room," I comment as we pass it, feeling my cheeks heat.

"What would you call it?" he questions and I change the subject before I find myself wanting to go inside of it—the wooden bench room—rather than hear him tell me more stories. It's the intellectual side of him I need to feel safe. Although his touch is just as addictive.

"You said you didn't used to use this gym," I comment, nodding my head toward the last door we passed on the left. The equipment looks virtually brand new.

"I didn't, but lately the other gym has... The women seem to like the main gym."

"The women?" My eyebrow raises on its own.

"Chloe, Addison, Aria, they live in the estate with us. You'll meet them soon, I think."

I don't anticipate the pressure that overwhelms me at the thought. As we walk down the hall toward the foyer which leads to the door separating this wing from the rest of the estate, I drag my fingertips along the wall. All the while thinking how close he must be to his brothers since they live together. Only a hall away.

"So they... they get how it is?" I ask him, watching

my feet and wondering if they feel the same way as I do. "Chloe, Addison and…"

"And Aria. Yes. They grew up in this life. They aren't like you." I can't explain why it hurts so much to hear him say it like that. *Not like me.*

"They're your brothers' girlfriends?" I'm quick to keep up the conversation and not let on how I'm feeling.

"No. Declan is single. He's happy being on his own."

"No one's really happy being on their own." I didn't mean to say that out loud.

"You were alone for a long time," he notes.

"I had my work."

"That's still alone."

"I didn't say I was happy." My rebuttal is quick and unfortunate. I'd rather talk about his brothers.

"So one of the three women is…"

It only takes two more steps and a side-eye for Jase to tell me that Chloe is Sebastian's wife and remind me that I met him in the kitchen the other day.

"Right." I nod and try to picture his face again, but I can't. It seems like most of Jase's family has their own little family. I like that. I don't know why I do, but it makes me feel safer still. "What about Seth?"

"He doesn't have a girl… that I know of. I think he has other things in mind," he answers cryptically.

"What do you mean?"

"He's been off."

With a cocked brow, I motion for him to continue.

"He's seeing someone, that's obvious enough. I just don't know who."

"You could ask him."

"That's not the way I go about things."

"Aren't you friends?" Of everyone I've met, Seth's the only person I had mentally filed as a friend of Jase.

"I trust him to the point where it would be hard to think…" He doesn't finish his thought but before I can pry he speaks again. "I don't really have friends, but I'm friendly with him."

"How did you guys meet?"

"Push came to shove a few years back, and he was there, in a spot where he could have done a lot of things. Seth could have ended us—me and my brothers—before we really got started… all because I fucked up." He scratches the back of his neck and even though he's speaking so casually, his expression is hard and unforgiving.

"What did you do?"

"It was at The Red Room. We'd just opened and I let someone in who I shouldn't have. I showed him something that no one's supposed to see." An ominous tone tinges his last statement.

I whisper, "Are you going to tell me what?"

"A basement where I bring people to…"

"To kill." I finish the sentence so he doesn't have to.

"Yes, let's go with kill."

"And what happened?"

"The doors were open, the man saw and took off. None of us were armed as a show of faith, which was fucking stupid. Seth was out there in the parking lot, and he saw us running after him."

"Seth just happened to be there?" I question, not understanding.

"He'd stopped by The Red Room that night, wanting

to work with us. We told him no. He came back at just the right time."

"Why couldn't you work with him?"

"He was too… he was too big, too set in his ways. He came from a town where he was the person everyone went to. I don't need someone looking over my shoulder, someone wanting to take command."

"Too many chefs, so to speak."

"Something like that. Anyway, that night he saw, and he could have let the fucker take off. He didn't."

I've been to The Red Room enough to imagine someone bolting from the doors. The forest is close; the highway is even closer. It wouldn't take much to get away if only you got past the parking lot.

"After helping us take care of the body, he told me, *'If you change your mind, I'm good at taking direction,'* or something like that."

"And that convinced you?" I ask him.

"We would have been done if that asshole had gotten out and told the feds what he saw; it turned out that he was undercover. We didn't have the police back then on our payroll. We didn't have much protection. Things were harder then and we needed the help. That's really what it comes down to."

"So you aren't friends then. Simply coworkers who rely on each other?"

"He's more of a friend to Declan. They're closer than we are."

It's quiet as we come to the stairwell and he tells me the upstairs is mostly unfinished. He's never had a reason to complete it.

Taking my hand, he lets his middle finger trail down the lines in my palm. There's a hint of charm and flirtation I'm not expecting. One that breaks the tension, scattering it in any and all directions until it's gone.

"I like touching you," he says faintly.

Something about the ease he feels around me makes me want to stay by him forever. I'm so aware of it in this moment.

So aware, that it's frightening. With every breadcrumb of information Jase gives me, I fall deeper in love with him. Even if the pieces are perverse and disturbing… maybe more so because of it. Even if I wake up tonight like I have the past few nights, breathless and covered with a cold sweat, dreaming about the darkness I know is inside of him… even then. The fear is still there, but love is stronger. Which is why I'd fall back asleep next to him, willing my eyelids to shut and show me something sweeter.

"Ask me something," Jase offers.

The memories of everything that's happened flicker through my mind as I search for a question, and one is most apparent. A detail I've yet to tell him.

"Do you know anyone who wears white sneakers with a red stripe down the sides?"

His brow pulls together as he turns to look at me. "Why?" he asks.

I have to pull my hand away, feeling too hot, yet cold at the same time to tell him.

"When my house was broken into, that's all I saw from where I was hiding in the cabinet."

"White sneakers with a red stripe?" he clarifies.

"Right down the center, from front to back on the sides."

"Why haven't you told me this sooner? Is it all you saw? You're sure?" The questions hold an edge to them. Not anger, not resentment, more like an edge of failure and I hate it.

"I'm sorry... I just didn't know."

"You didn't know if you could trust me." He completes the statement for me and I nod. "I'm sorry," is all I can say, feeling like I've failed him.

With his hand brushing against my jaw, I lean into his touch and close my eyes, reveling in it.

"If I could start our story over and start it differently, I would. I want you to know that."

There's so much I'd change if I could. But then I wonder what our story would look like if it hadn't started so intensely.

"How many women have you done this to?"

"Done what?" he asks.

"Brought back here. Showed off this place to... told your deepest, darkest secrets?"

"None. You're the only one, cailín tine." His nickname for me still makes my stomach do little flips in a way that excites me.

"You've never called anyone else that?" I tease him and he nips my neck in admonishment while wrapping his hands around my waist and letting them slip lower.

"Never. You're my only fiery girl."

He's so consumed with lust in the moment, but there's something nagging at me, something that feels off.

"Why don't I believe you?" My question pulls him out of the moment.

"Because you see my sins, however many of them, and you've judged me guilty of them all." The honesty of it stares back at me from the depths of his dark eyes. "If you'll lie, you'll cheat… if you'll cheat…" He doesn't continue and I bring my lips to his even though pain etches its way between us. "Even a saint has to start somewhere… I'll never be a saint though. If I could change for you, change this life, this world, our pasts, I would. But it's not going to happen. I can't start our story over."

I kiss him again, feeling the heat between us, feeling his hard lips soften as I press mine against his. I finally answer him, "I know." And then remind him, "I'm not asking you to."

When Jase tries to take me back to his bedroom, I tell him no. Instead I lead him to the plush rug in his office that's not an office. I ask him to light the fire and I slowly undress, watching both hunger and flames in his eyes once the fire's ignited.

I pick the knife I want him to use on me and I lie down without a weighted blanket at my feet, without cuffs, without rope this time, although I tell him I miss the rough feeling when it's all over.

We're both moths to each other's flames, ignited by our touch. We're drawn together, destroyed together. It used to scare me, but there's no fighting it. *Isn't that what love is?*

You can say chemistry was never our problem. Take away the drugs, his brothers, the feeling of loss and betrayal, and all that's left is the simple truth that's he's mine and I'm his. In the most primitive way, we make perfect sense. We're drawn to one another in a way where nothing else matters. It all fades to a blur when I stare into his eyes.

But that's where the problem truly lies. He wasn't meant for my world and I wasn't meant for his. Everything else matters with him in a world where every step is dangerous, and we should have accounted for that. I'll never be able to escape Jase Cross or his merciless world.

This attraction will never allow it.

Jase

The light of the fire dances across her skin in the darkness, and the shadows from the flame beckon me to touch her. The sight of the dip in her waist is an image that would start wars. Her breathing is steady in her deep sleep and part of me wants to leave her here, resting on her side on the luxurious rug with the only covers being the warmth of the raging fire. The other part wants to have her again in my bed.

The low hum of a vibration steals my attention. My muscles stretch with a beautiful pain as I pull myself away from Bethany and get my phone. Still naked and still hungry for more of her and the promise of keeping her here, I check my messages.

It's a text from Seth, just the person I need to speak with.

Anger has a way of destroying the calm, even when Bethany stirs with a feminine sigh in her sleep. Her hand reaches right where I just was and it seals her fate.

I text Seth back. *Meet me first thing tomorrow. We have things to discuss.*

CHAPTER 9

Bethany

It only takes one deep breath in the massive kitchen and a long stretch of my back to release the tension from last night. Things are better. It feels like a huge step forward, but something's still holding me back. The nightmares haven't stopped; they've only changed.

Last night, my mother reminded me that everyone I loved would die before me and that it was okay. It's not the first time I've dreamed about being back at the home, with my mother looking me directly in the eyes and telling me what felt like a message from death. The terror gripped me the same way she did all those years ago. It was like I was back there, but not really. We were on my porch and I couldn't move. I couldn't speak either. My sister came to help me, ripping our mother away and yelling at her, screaming at her. It was so unlike her, but somehow I believed it.

When they were done fighting with each other, my sister turned to me and looked me in the eyes. She said my mother was right. They would all die before me.

That's when I woke up. At 5:00 a.m. in the morning, in an empty bed that held the faint, masculine scent of Jase Cross.

I can walk around pretending I'm not uneasy, but I've never been good with pretending.

As my gaze falls to the slick counters and I hear the thump of footsteps getting louder, cuing someone's incoming arrival, I put away my thoughts of my family, or what used to be family.

Carter's deep voice reverberates in the expansive space. "Bethany."

His gaze is narrowed and even harsh. Even the air around him warns me not to mess with the man. Some men are just like that; the feel of danger comes with their strong posture and chiseled jaw.

"Cross," I answer him tersely with a cocked brow.

I find myself comparing him to Jase, but even though they look alike, Jase is nothing like him. He's charming and approachable in a way I don't think I'll ever find Carter to be.

An asymmetric grin pulls at his lips. "Funny you should call me Cross when you're with my brother and he's also a Cross."

"Suits you though."

He huffs a short chuckle and lets the smile grow as I pull the fridge door open, searching for a can of Coke or something with caffeine in it. "Something funny?" I ask him.

There's a case of Dr. Pepper and the hint of a smile appears on my face too. It's been a while since I've had one of these and they're in glass bottles... that makes it even better.

"You aren't the only one who thinks that."

"Thinks what?" I ask him genuinely, already forgetting what I'd said before as I'm too distracted by my beverage.

"Nothing." He shrugs it off and goes to the cabinet, pulling out a box of tea bags and a pretty mug with owls on it. I nearly tease him, taunt him for the girly mug, even though I know it must be for his wife. I bite my tongue and stifle the playful thoughts as I prepare to go somewhere else and stay out of Carter's way. This isn't my house and he isn't my family. I'm more than aware of that.

I only get one step away though before Carter speaks with his back to me, putting a mug of water in the microwave. "Spring will be here soon," he tells me.

Stopping in my tracks, I turn rather than look over my shoulder and wait for him to turn as well. He does slowly, awkwardly even with his broad shoulders.

"Why does your face look like that?" he asks me when he takes in what must be a confused expression.

"Is that your attempt at small talk?"

"People like to talk about the weather, Miss Fawn."

It's my turn to let out a huff of a laugh, small and insignificant, but it breaks the tension, one chisel at a time.

"Spring's my favorite season."

"It's Aria's too. Well," he continues talking as he retrieves the mug from the now beeping microwave and sets a bag of tea into the cup. "Spring and fall. She said she can't pick just one."

It doesn't pass my notice that his expression softens when he talks about Aria. The recollection softens something inside of me too.

"How long have you and Aria been together?"

"Just a little while." His answer is... less than informative. Maybe it's a Cross brothers thing.

"I heard she's expecting?"

"That's right." His grin turns cocky and I half expect him to brag about how it happened on the first try or how his swimmers are so strong. Some macho bullshit like that, but it doesn't come.

"Congratulations."

"Thank you."

"Well, I'll let you get to it," I tell him, but he doesn't let the conversation end.

"Jase really likes you." The statement surprises me, holding me where I am.

Warmth flows through me, from my chest all the way to my cheeks. I don't know what to say other than, "I really like him too."

"He's turning back to his emotional... hotheaded younger self."

"Hotheaded?" I pry. Carter doesn't seem to take the bait though.

"When we were younger, he used to be a real troublemaker," Carter says as he leans against the counter, staring into the cup of tea and lifting the bag of leaves. We both watch the steam billow into a swirl of dissipating clouds although I'm across the room.

"Really?" The shock is evident.

"Not because he was... like me. Not that kind of trouble."

If Carter's going to talk, I'm damn well going to listen. Taking a step closer to the counter, I ask him, "What kind of trouble?"

He peers at me, but not for long. "He just couldn't keep his mouth shut. It should have gotten him into more trouble than it did really. I know if I'd done it... My father never hit Jase. I can't remember a single time. He liked the belt and took it out on us mostly, me and Daniel."

A sadness creeps inside of me at the ease with which Carter speaks of his father beating him and his brother. He was the oldest. I'm the youngest, but I remember the way my mother used to yell at my sister for things that I didn't even think were wrong. With parted lips, I grip the edge of the counter, cold and unmoving as he continues. "I remember so many times my father would say to Jase, *your mouth is going to get you in trouble.*"

"Parents sometimes take it out on the eldest."

"If I'd talked like Jase did when we were younger, I'd have been punched in the mouth." Carter's statement doesn't come with emotion. It's merely the way things were for them back then.

"He used to say it like it was. He never had a filter, and couldn't just be quiet. There were so many times he said shit to my father that made my back arch expecting to be hit there. He had the balls to call everyone out on their shit and never stopped for a moment to question what he was saying."

"Honesty without compassion is brutality." I say the quote and then add when Carter looks back at me, "I don't know who said it. It's just a saying."

Standing up straighter, he holds the tea with both

hands and tells me, "He was compassionate, too much. That's why he never let a moment pass him where he thought he could change what was happening if he only made people aware of how wrong it was."

It's hard to keep my expression straight. I can only imagine Jase as a young boy, watching everything that happened and speaking up, expecting it to help, when there was never any help coming.

"He used to have hope." My first statement is quiet and I think it goes unheard so I raise my voice. "It sounds like he was a good kid," I comment and Carter's forehead wrinkles with amusement.

"Sure, as good as the Cross boys could ever be."

"You know," I start to say, and that stops him from walking off while I tap the glass base of my Dr. Pepper on the counter. "My sister was like that. When I was growing up and she was in high school and even part of college, she was a lot like that."

"Is that right?" he asks, leaning against one of the stools and listening to my story.

"When our mom got sick, she had Alzheimer's." I have to take a quick sip as the visions of my sister, a younger, healthier version, flood into my mind. Jenny would stand outside the university before every football game and every council meeting with flyers she'd printed from the library. "My sister wanted to educate people. She said it might help them because if you can diagnose it early, it can lessen the symptoms."

I'll never forget how often Jenny stood there after mom was diagnosed. I met her outside the stadium one chilly October night. She had a handful of flyers and tearstained cheeks. She'd been there every night that week, and I wanted her to come home. I needed help. *Mom* needed help.

When I told her to come home, she broke down and cried. She didn't want to go home to a mother who didn't know who she was. She said she blamed herself, because she knew something was wrong and she hadn't said anything. She did nothing when she could have at least spoken up like she would have before she was busy with classes.

All the while she spent her nights standing there, I did what was practical. I listened to Nurse Judy, I figured out the bills and how to pay them all with what we had. I took care of the house and learned how to help any way I could.

My sister looked backward, while I tried to look forward. I think that's where the difference really lay.

"That doesn't sound like mouthing off," Carter comments.

"Maybe that wasn't the best example," I answer under my breath, not seeing the similarity so clearly like I did a moment ago. I find myself lacking, not unlike the way I felt back then. The visions of her that night she cried on the broken sidewalk don't leave me.

"She blames herself then?" Carter asks and I have to blink away the memories.

"Yeah, she did. Blamed," I correct him. "She passed away this past month."

Something strange happens then. The air in the room turns cold and distant as Carter looks away from me.

Some people deal with death differently, but it's odd the way he reacts. He doesn't look back at me. He stares off down the hall and past the kitchen toward his wing of the estate, avoiding my prying gaze.

"I'm sorry," he finally speaks, although he pays close attention to the mug in his hand. His lips part but only to inhale slightly; I think he's going to say more but he doesn't. And then it's silent again.

I don't like it. The little hairs on the back of my neck stand to attention and the uneasiness I felt when I walked into the kitchen greets me again.

"When she died, I inherited her debt and met your brother, so if nothing else..." My voice trails off. *What the fuck am I even saying?*

It's hard to swallow, but I force down a sip of the cold drink and let the taste settle on the back of my tongue where the words all hide. *At least her death led me to Jase.*

Was I really thinking that?

Was I really drawing a positive out of my sister's murder?

"A debt? Did Jase help you out of something?" Carter's dark eyes seek mine and I reach them instantly. Suddenly he's interested.

"The debt my sister owed," I state, feeling a line draw across my forehead as I read his expression. No memory is worn there of the money she owed the Cross brothers. Money Jenny owed to Carter.

Jase blamed Carter, didn't he? He said Carter wouldn't let it go even if Jase wanted to.

"Who did she owe money to?" Carter asks and the wind leaves my lungs in a heavy pull. Drawn from me so violently, that I drop the bottle to the counter with a hard clink.

Jase lied. Staring into Carter's clueless eyes, I see it so clearly now.

He lied to me about the debt.

About my sister owing it.

I thought so poorly of her. That she would owe so much money to men like him.

And he put that on her.

With a sudden twist, my gut wrenches with sickness and I have to focus on breathing just to keep from losing it.

He lied to me. It was all a lie.

How can I believe anything that comes out of his mouth? How many lies has he told me? How many things has he kept from me?

"Where are you going?" Carter's voice carries down the hall, chasing after me and I ignore him. I don't trust myself to speak.

Every step hurts more and more. I've fallen for him. That's the only explanation for the way my face crumples as I storm off. The way my eyes feel hot although there's no fucking way I'll cry. I won't cry for a man who lies to my face over and over again.

I let him touch me. I let him use me. Because he lied about a debt.

I'm foolish. I'm a stupid little girl in his man's world.

"I hate him." The words tumble out in a single breath as my hands form fists. I hate that I believed him. That I fell for him.

No… no I don't. My throat dries at the realization.

I hate that I wanted him to treat me like he loves me. I hate that I believed he did.

You don't lie to the ones you care for. You don't use them.

You don't coerce them and blackmail them.

I thought he loved me though.

Maybe he still does... the small voice whispers. The voice that's gotten me deeper and deeper into bed with a man who tells me lies. A voice I wish would speak louder, because I desperately want it to be speaking the truth. But the rest of me knows it's a childish wish, that I need to grow the fuck up and slap the shit out of Jase's lying mouth.

CHAPTER 10

Jase

"What did he say specifically?" I question Seth, comparing notes.

"To meet… to come alone… and that he has evidence he doesn't want to use against us."

Our pace is even as I walk with him from the foyer to the office. I waited for him outside after taking Bethany to bed last night. Watching the late dusk turn to fog in the early morning and preparing for what has to happen today.

I respond, "Officer Walsh is my new favorite person to hate."

"Do you think it has to do with Jenny?" he asks.

"I doubt it. If he has something on us and if he's going to use it to blackmail us…" My teeth clench hard as I release an agitated exhale.

"Do you think you should tell Bethany? In case this leads to something?"

"No." Shaking my head, I think about the way Bethany's going to react when she finds out about her sister being alive and the fact that I knew this whole time. "I want to know I'll be able to bring her back before I tell her anything."

"Marcus will know when we find her. I don't see how he won't know when we approach. Unless it's only a few of us, but that would be suicide."

"We'll all go. He can know. I would think he already knows we've been watching."

He stops walking and the sound of two men walking down a long hall turns to one and then none as I turn to him, waiting for him to speak.

"You think Marcus would go against us?"

"I don't know," I answer him honestly and feel a chill run up my spine. The silver glimmer of the scar on my knuckles shines in the dim hall lighting. "We've never openly been against him, but he's never taken from us either. He has her. He knows we want her back. It was his call to decide that and ours to decide the consequence."

"We don't know that. We don't know how it happened and what she's doing with him."

"There's too much we don't know, but we don't have time to wait. If we find their lookout point or storage centers, or anything at all, we go in." My words are final and Seth's slight nod is in agreement.

With a tilt of his chin, we continue back to the office. Every step I take grows heavier, and the anxiousness of getting down to what we have to discuss stifles the air and coils every muscle in my body.

I force myself to stay calm with my hand on the doorknob to my office, careful not to say anything until he walks in first.

"Did you get it?" I ask him as I flick on the light. It's still early morning and the sky's a dark gray. Pulling back the curtains, the harsh sound of them opening is the only thing to be heard as Seth walks to the row of books on the other side of the room.

Clouds cover the sky, hanging thick and with varied shades of gray. Rain's coming and with it, a darkness that will cover the day.

"I did," he tells me, leaving a book he's eyeing to come to stand where I am and hand me the box.

"What do you think?" I ask him.

"I agree with you," he says simply. "It's why I like working for you."

As I'm inspecting it, he delivers news I didn't think would come so soon. "There may be a room, or tunnel, or shelter of some kind."

He leans his back against the leather chaise, crossing his arms in front of his chest. "The blueprints for the bridge don't show anything. So what's under the bridge is… we don't know."

"You're sure of it?"

He bows his head in acknowledgment. "We've kept an eye on the people associated with Jenny being taken. They're out there, making these rounds and going to the same spots. Last night, one disappeared. Nik was watching him, and then he was gone. There has to be some hideout there we haven't yet found."

Slipping the box into my pocket, I ask him, "Did he do surveillance?"

"Not yet." Uncrossing his arms, he slips his hands into his pants pockets and glances at the unlit fireplace before turning back to me. "I wasn't sure how you wanted to proceed."

"You seem distracted," I tell him, rather than giving orders. It could be a setup. It could be suicide. Carter should know before we decide anything.

"Me?" he questions.

"You didn't think I'd noticed?"

His answer is to tilt his head. With a cluck of his tongue, he pushes off the chaise and walks to the bookshelf before confiding in me. "We're distracted for the same reasons, I think."

Every hair stands on end at the thought of him being distracted by Bethany. The skin across my knuckles stretches and turns white as I crack them with my thumb, one by one and consciously resist forming a fist.

"What reason is that?" I ask and my voice is low.

"A girl."

"Bethany?" I question and now my tone is threatening.

"She's yours and I have mine."

"So you are seeing someone?" I ask him and the edge of jealousy seeps away, although not as easily as it came.

Instead of answering, he suggests, "You should take Bethany to the graveyard. I think it'd be good for you two."

"You're good at distraction," I comment as I eye him moving down the rows of books he's seen before.

"You go there often…" he pauses before continuing, seeming to struggle with how he wants to say what's on his mind. Choosing a new book, one I recognize by the distinctive spine, he tells me, "I almost took her there when I picked her up a few days ago. Thought you could meet her there, but then I got your message."

"Why would she want to go there?"

"She's empathetic. She reacts to emotion. If she saw the end result of what you've been through… it makes things more real. To see loss."

"She knows what a graveyard looks like. She's been there herself a time or two."

"She hasn't though. She didn't go to her sister's funeral. I don't know about her mother's either. She was working a lot back then."

The fact that Seth knows this and I don't makes me feel a certain way; I hate him for it, but I'm grateful for the message. We work differently, we see things differently. I could have never imagined it'd work so well for so long.

"I have to tell you something before I forget." Tapping my fingers along the hard walnut shelves, I let my gaze stray down the shelves. "You need to get rid of your shoes."

"What?" His surprise is met with a huff of humor. "Now you're going with the distraction method," he jokes although he's still waiting for me to explain what the hell I'm talking about.

"The ones you wore when you went to check on Bethany. When she thought there was a break-in."

"I don't even know what shoes they were."

"White with red stripes on the sides," I answer him and finally make my way to take a seat. "She saw them, so it's best to get rid of them." As I sit down, I focus on the box, thinking about it rather than Seth and the fact that Bethany saw his shoes.

"Fuck." Seth closes the book in his hand with a thwack,

lowering his head and shaking it. "That could have ended badly."

"If she didn't tell me, I imagine it would have if she'd seen you in them."

"Are you going to tell her it was Marcus or Romano or some random burglars or what?"

"She's too smart to think it was random." Leaning my head back, I close my eyes and hate the way all this started. "I don't know," I answer him. "One fucking lie after the next with her."

A creaking sound snaps my eyes to the open door of the office. The dim light behind her places a shadow of contempt across her hurt gaze and pouty lips. Her small hands are balled into fists gripping the hem of her gray sweater. Even enraged, she's in pain. It's etched into every detail of her. *Fuck.*

"Bethany." Her name tumbles from my mouth as I stand up, feeling the thrum of disaster in my blood.

Chapter 11

Bethany

"I can explain," Jase repeats as he rounds the worn leather chair. Through my blurry vision I can barely make out Seth backing away from both of us as I stalk into the room.

I'm shaking, trembling, on the verge of a rage I didn't know was possible.

"I hate you," I sneer and how my words come out so clearly, I'll never know. They strike him, visibly, across the face as he stops with both hands up a foot away from me.

"What did you hear?" he asks me calmly and I want to spit at him. I can already see him spinning a new lie in his head, just waiting to know what I heard so he can manipulate it. Betrayal is a nasty thing, twisting a knife deeper into my rib cage.

All I can remember is how I felt standing in the

threshold of my kitchen, too afraid to speak or move, and knowing I had nowhere to run. "It was Seth? It was your men all along?"

My vision blurs with the present and the past.

"I sent him to check on you. I was with Carter and Aria; I couldn't come so I sent Seth."

"Seth crept into my house. It was Seth." I repeat it and I still can't believe it. I can't believe it's true.

"He was only going to stay with you because I thought someone was threatening you--"

"Someone?" I question, feeling raging tremors run through me. Even now, he hides from me.

"It doesn't matter--"

"The fuck it doesn't!" I scream out of nowhere, shocking both of us.

"It's all right." I can hear Seth but I don't dare rip my eyes away from Jase.

"Get out," Jase gives his partner in crime the command and I listen to his heavy footsteps as he leaves. I can't even look him in the face. He didn't come just to stay with me, that's bullshit. It's all bullshit.

"Who?" I demand.

"Marcus." Jase's chest rises higher and falls deeper, moving slower as he tries to stay calm and collected. I take a step to my right, and he takes a step to his left.

"So you sent your men?"

"Seth said you weren't there, that you took off or something happened. So I sent every man I had."

"He didn't knock. He didn't try calling me or saying my name when he walked in." Shaking my head, I deny the innocence that he's trying to portray.

"He thought he may have frightened you into hiding."

I complete the series of events for him. "You thought that would be good. Scare me into your arms." My glare lifts to the specks of gold in his dark eyes. "You thought it would be easier to convince me, didn't you?"

I can hear the deep inhale he takes as he sucks in a breath. "I made a mistake."

"*One fucking lie after the next with her.*" I repeat the words he used before he knew I was outside the door with a taunting flourish. "How many lies, Jase?"

He doesn't answer me; he merely steps closer. "Can you even remember how many you told?" My voice gets louder with each question. Still, he doesn't answer.

"How about the debt? I just found out Carter never knew about it."

Jase doesn't react, he doesn't falter, still hiding behind a hard façade.

"Are you going to say there was truth to that? That my sister did what? What do you want to say she did, what did she do to rack up that debt? Tell me all the horrible things she did."

I can't explain how the pain flows; the best way to describe it is to say it's like a river flowing over jagged rocks. "You'll never know how much it hurt me to think she'd done something horrible to have a debt like that." I can't even speak the sentence clearly as I brace myself on the furniture.

"I'm sorry."

"So it was a lie too?"

"Yes."

"And the break-in? It was all you all along?"

"Yes."

With heated cheeks and a prick at the back of my eyes, I remember how I fell out of the cabinet that night and called for him. I remember how awful I felt the next day for ever thinking poorly of him.

How stupid I was. All I am with him is a step behind and foolish.

"You held me after. You *knew* and you held me after." I feel sick. My body leans to the left as my head spins and the bastard dares to reach for me.

"Get the fuck off," I say as I shove him away with every ounce of strength I have. It does nothing but push me backward, hitting the chaise and brushing my elbow against the leather. "Stay the fuck away from me," I grit out with disdain, pointing a finger at his chest.

He walks right into it. My finger is now touching his chest.

It's the lack of respect for my boundaries. This is the last fucking time I let him disrespect me.

His chest is like a brick wall, hard and unmoving, even after I slam my fist into it. My throat feels raw as I scream and the sides of my hands spasm with agony as I beat them against his chest over and over. "Get away from me!" Tears stream down my face in an oh-so-familiar path.

I hate it. I hate it all.

I hate the way it hurts. I hate that he did it.

I hate that I know he'd do it again, no matter how much he insists that he'd start the story over if he could. He'd do it the same way each and every time, because he doesn't trust me to love him.

"I hate you," I scream at him and his idiocy. "Stay away from me!"

Jase doesn't try to hold me back or stop me. He simply watches me lose it. The look on his face is one I recognize and it only makes my heart hurt more.

When our patients don't want to admit they're not okay but they're struggling to do anything at all we tell them, sometimes you have to break. You have to let it out, you have to feel it, you have to move through it even if you're a sobbing mess the entire time.

Sometimes a good cry or screaming session to let the anger and sorrow out is unavoidable.

Sometimes you have to break, even if you know you won't be put back together when you get to the other side of it all.

My body feels heavy as I drop to the floor on my knees. Struggling with the weight of it all. I can feel his hands on me, his grip to stay close to him, but I ignore it.

How many times have I held on to someone just as Jase is and told them to do it, to let it all out? To break apart. Not because you want to, not even to make anything better. Simply because you have to.

"You're a monster." The statement swells as it leaves me, strangling me as it goes.

Still, Jase holds on to my wrists.

The smooth wood is cold and I just want to lay my heated face against it. To let it all out, but Jase is there, not leaving me alone.

"I had to," he says and the statement is stretched with desperation.

I can barely swallow at this point, let alone speak.

There's no use fighting his grip on me; he's stronger. There's no use trying to wipe my eyes, since the tears keep coming.

"I didn't mean to hurt you," he whispers once I've stopped altogether, just feeling every piece of me shatter.

He didn't mean to, but he did it anyway.

"I didn't want to lie to you," he says and his voice is calming as he brings me into his lap.

He didn't want to, yet he did.

A heave of sorrow erupts from inside of me as I realize I didn't want to love him, but I did. I didn't want to trust him, but I did.

"There are very few things that a person has to do," I whisper against his shirt, staring at the crack of light under the door. "You *chose* to do that to me. You *chose* to lie and scare me to get me to do what you wanted. You *chose* to manipulate me."

The gentle rocking is paused and it's then that I realize how hot I am, leaning against him and I try to pull away. This time he lets me.

The irony is that all he had to do was ask or even tell me. I was so desperate for someone and something. Him scaring me had nothing to do with it. "You didn't have to do it."

"I told you, I told you if I could start it over, I would." His voice is low, but has an edge of anguish.

"You didn't tell me why though," I say and lift my head to look him in the eyes, finding my own reflection staring back at me. Crumpled and weak, just how he sees me. "You didn't tell me it's because you lied to me every step of the way."

"There are reasons."

"There's no reason good enough."

"I couldn't let you go."

"It's not your decision to make." Every response from me turns colder and more absolute. Inside I'm on fire, the blaze of hate destroying everything that made me feel alive with Jase Cross. It rages in my mind, changing the memories, making me feel like they weren't real.

It was all a lie.

"You wanted me to marry you and weeks ago you fed me one lie after another so I'd do what you want."

"Bethany," he pleads with me.

"I told you I loved you and you made me feel like you loved me too." My brow pinches together as I wipe violently under my eyes. "How could you when you knew it was all a lie?"

"Bethany, don't. It's not like that--"

"But it is! That's exactly what it's like!"

Placing both of his hands on my shoulder, he tries to console me as if he's the man who should be doing that. "It's over with now, it's better now."

"I never want to see you again." As I speak the words, my heart splits in two. I feel it slice cleanly, seemingly fine, then bleeding out in a single beat. "I have to protect myself and you keep hurting me. You won't stop." I hate that my bottom lip wobbles. I hate that I believe what I'm saying. I hate that it's the truth. "If you need me to behave some type of way, you'll lie to me. You'll pull strings and make me do what you say."

My head shakes at the idea, hating what he's done and wanting to deny it; Jase's shakes on its own, but for different reasons I imagine, because he knows I'm telling the truth. I'm not the one who's lied. Feeling my resolve, I push myself up off the floor, ready to leave him. Preparing to piece myself back together and lick my wounds, but he stops me with one statement.

"Marcus has Jenny." Jase's voice is low, the words coming from deep in his chest.

Jenny?

"How dare you." I have no air in my lungs. No will to do anything but slap him. Hard and fast, leaving a red mark and forcing his head to whip to the side. "You don't get to use her against me. You don't get to manipulate me with her *ever again!*" I scream in his face and then clench my teeth together when he grabs my wrists as he pins me to him, restraining my elbows so I can't hit him, so I can't move. All I can do is look in his eyes.

"She's still alive, Bethany," he whispers and it's so compelling.

I want nothing more than to believe him. To believe the liar who's already brought shame to her memory.

"She's dead." A fresh flood of tears threatens to fall, but I won't let him see them. He doesn't get to be there for me. Not again. I pull away from his grasp, ripping my arm away so I can free myself.

The bright red handprint against his cheek is still there. "She's alive. We have a video of her with a man after the funeral. After the trunk was discovered."

"With Marcus?" I can barely remain upright. She's alive. I'm so cold. A freezing wave flows over my skin. *She's alive.*

Hope makes my body tremble.

"A different man. He's dead, but we have an idea where he's keeping her."

"Where who is keeping her?"

"Marcus."

I'm so confused, so consumed by questions, but one begs to be answered. "How long have you known?"

Silence. The silence is my answer.

"I have never hated you more," I speak when he doesn't. Swallowing thickly and feeling a spiked ball form in my throat, I continue. "You saw what that did to me. How could you watch me mourn her death…" I have to stop and breathe in deep.

"Because I love you… I didn't want to tell you if I couldn't save her."

"So you can save her now?" I question him, focused on my sister before realizing what he said.

I love you.

"You're telling me all this now because we've fallen apart." I speak the unforgiving truth. "Not because you can save her." *And not because you truly love me.* I keep that bit to myself.

"I'm trying. We have a plan. I didn't want to tell you until I knew for sure."

"You're sure she's alive?" Jenny. My sister's face plays in my mind and I have to cover my own. *Please, God. Let her be alive.*

"As of two weeks ago, yes."

Two weeks. Two weeks is so long. Too long. Please, God.

"Will you save her for me?" I beg him, looking up at him and praying for him to do just that. Even if he doesn't love me. Even if he lies to me a million times more until the day I can see her again. "I'll do anything," I confess and my voice cracks.

"I'm doing my best. It's the first time we've ever tracked anything that has to do with Marcus."

I have never felt more at his mercy and more alone than in this moment. I don't know what to believe or what to do. It's too much.

"I'm breaking, Jase. I can feel myself slowly breaking down and I can't stop it. Don't take advantage of me. Don't do this to me. I'm not okay."

"I'm not taking advantage of you."

"Then don't say you love me if you really don't. It's not fair. Because I do love you. I hate you right now and we're not okay, but I love you." I don't know how I'm even able to speak, since the sudden rush of emotions are warring with each other at the back of my throat.

Jase struggles to hide his as well. "I don't love you, is that what you want to hear?"

"Don't do that. Don't use what we used to have." My finger raises as I yell at him, my voice cracking. *He loves me.*

Heaving in a breath with the intensity growing in his eyes his own voice trembles as he says, "Whether you believe it or not, I love you and you're staying here."

With an exhale and then another, a calmer one, his expression softens as he waits for me. He's waiting for me to say it again and I know he is. "Everything I've done is for you. I love you, cailín tine."

"I don't want you to call me that right now." I stop him with the statement, not knowing what to believe. Adrenaline is coursing through my body. Fight or flight taking over. He won't let me leave and he's the only one left to fight. "Of everything I learned today, the only thing that I can focus on right now is that my sister is still alive."

"I know. And I'm here for you." He tries again to appeal

to the side of me that's still holding on to hope for us. I'm ashamed to admit that side still exists.

"How could you watch me cry for her and accept her death when you knew she was alive? I can't even stomach the thought."

"I'm sorry."

"Do you expect to say you're sorry and I simply forgive you?" I throw his own words back in his face. "Words are meaningless."

"You can't leave me when we fight." He says the words like they're a truth that's undeniable. Like nothing else matters.

"Lying to me isn't the same as fighting. And what you lied about… I'm not okay." Pulling away from him, I feel the chill in the air. "Nothing about this is okay."

My legs feel weak when I stand and he tries to right me, but I do it myself.

"I'm going to the guest room." I give him my final words. The only ones I have for him in this moment. "Don't lock me in and don't trap me. But leave me the hell alone for right now."

Loneliness is a horrible companion, but it's the one I need right now. I think about messaging Laura, but I'm still pissed at her. Instead, I sit on the bed and look out of the window. Just to think. Just to break down again. All alone.

Does he know the nightmares he's given me? The hate I feel for myself knowing I'd said goodbye to my sister, even though I still felt her presence. I knew I shouldn't have, that it was too soon.

Shame is what comes for me when the loneliness no longer matters.

I don't hear the door open and I don't hear Seth walk in until he speaks from across the room. "Are you all right?"

Lifting my head from my folded arms, I glance over my shoulder. I'm certain I look like a wreck, with my knees pulled into my chest so I'm merely a ball of limbs staring out a window.

"What do you think?" I ask him.

"I know you hate me--"

"I don't hate you."

"Well, I know you're mad at me, and I'm sorry."

"Okay." The petty answer leaves me instantly. I'll be damned if I'm simply going to forgive him in this moment.

The bed dips and I turn back to Seth, warning him to get the hell out. "I'd like to be alone."

"Just one thing." Although it's a statement, he says it like it's a question.

With a nod, I agree to hear him out.

"He lied to you, he does that," Seth tells me easily, like there's nothing wrong at all with it. "He made mistakes he's not used to. He decided to do things he shouldn't have." There's a rhythm to his voice that's calming. I fall for it, listening to every word he says. "He's not the only person I've ever met that lies to make other people feel better."

"He could say he's sorry," I counter as if a simple "sorry" would make much of a difference. Then I remember... he did. He said he was sorry. I don't remember for which part. Maybe all of it. He was right though, words are meaningless.

"He's not. He'd do it again if he had to." I'd be pissed off if Seth wasn't so matter of fact and if I wasn't so convinced already that what he's saying is the absolute truth.

"Then why should I ever trust him again?" That's really what it comes down to. I don't know that I can believe him or trust him ever again.

"Because he's trying to be a better man... for you. He's done all of this, *for you*."

I try to respond, to disagree. But I can't. Intention matters and behind all of this, he wanted to keep me safe. He tells me one last thing as he makes his way out.

"You know he loves you." Seth sounds so sure of it. "Just love him back." With that he shuts the door, not waiting for a response.

CHAPTER 12

Jase

"I'D SAY SHE'S PISSED," I COMMENT IN THE dark night as I shut my car door. I fucking hate that I'm not there now, just in case she wants to talk or yell... even if she wants to hit me again.

"I'd say she has a right to be." Glaring at Seth's profile, I note that he doesn't look back at me until he adds, "She loves you, though." When his eyes reach mine, I look ahead instead.

He changes the subject to ask, "You ready for this?"

It's bitter cold as the clear, glassy surface of the puddle beneath my boot is shattered. I don't hesitate to take another step and another. Moving quickly through the harsh wind to the warehouse.

"No one's ever ready for this shit."

"I don't like not knowing what to expect," Seth

comments, and it's only then that I notice how tense he seems.

"Whatever happens in there, we'll figure it out," I assure him. "Follow my lead."

"I'm not sure I'm the best at that, Boss."

"You've always been the best."

"Not at following… I like lists and control and knowing what to do. If you're telling me that you don't know, I'm telling you I might not follow."

There's always been direction. Always been a sense of right and wrong and a certain way to do things. Recently though, everything has been like walking through fog.

"Whatever you do," I finally answer him, "don't point your gun at me. Aim it at the prick who brought us here."

With a huff of a laugh he tells me, "I'll try to remember that."

Pushing open the double doors, I feel every muscle in my body coil, ready to act. Bright light greets us instantly, blinding me momentarily. It only makes the adrenaline in my blood pump harder and faster.

"We've been waiting for you." Officer Cody Walsh's voice reverberates in the large empty space. Blood rushes in my ears as I take in the man who's been like a dog with a bone ever since he arrived in town.

There's no back room or secret entrances in the empty warehouse. The ceilings have to be twenty feet high and the room itself is vacant, all 1200 square feet of it. With the exception of a steel shelf on the back wall and several stacks of old metal chairs behind Officer Walsh and another man I've never seen before, there's nothing here. Nowhere for anyone else to hide. That doesn't mean there aren't cameras.

"Good to see you again, Officer," I speak and other than my voice, the only sounds are the large fans spinning above us as we walk to them, slowly closing the distance. Seth stays back slightly, letting me lead the way.

Officer Walsh is in jeans and a black leather jacket, nothing like his typical attire, save the expression on his face.

"Undercover tonight?" Seth mutters beneath his breath, although it's a joke—there's a serious hint of a smirk there—and I share a quick glance with him. All of the FBI cases we could find on Walsh are sealed, except for one case. The one that has information on Marcus as well. His files were squeaky clean, with numerous medals and honors, referrals. But not a damn thing about undercover work. Anyone could spot him as a cop. He'd die in a week out here if he pulled that shit.

Our boots smack off the cement floor as my eyes adjust to the fluorescent lighting and we get closer to the two of them.

The other man is younger. Maybe in his thirties, or late twenties. In dark gray sweats and a long-sleeve black Henley, he would come off as relaxed if he didn't keep looking between Cody Walsh and the two of us.

"I don't think we've met," I address the other man, and the moment he opens his mouth to greet me, Officer Walsh whips up his gun to the side of the man's head and fires.

The racing of my heart isn't quite as fast as I am to pull my gun from its holster. With both hands on the steel in my hands, I stare at Walsh pointing the barrel at the unsuspecting man beside him. If Walsh sees my gun and Seth's aimed at him, he doesn't react, he only watches the man to his left. The dead man falls to his knees, his eyes dead and vacant with a rough bullet hole leaking blood down his face. Walsh continues to focus on him until finally, the man falls face-first onto the floor with a dull thud.

"I was wondering when you were going to get here so I could kill him," Walsh admits, his eyes watching the bright red blood pool around the nameless man's face.

Our pistols are still on him and he only seems to notice now.

"I wouldn't if I were you. If I don't make it back to the office and pull the tapes out of the mail room, all the evidence will be dispersed."

Seth's gaze sears into me. I can hear the soles of his shoes scrape against the ground as he shuffles his feet although his gun is still up.

Keeping myself calm, I lower the gun and shrug as if I'm unaffected. "I didn't take you for a man who liked the dramatic."

Officer Walsh is a man who's strictly by the book. That's everything we found on him. Clean record and a man who believes in black and white with no grays in between. This… this is to throw us off. It can't be his normal.

"I didn't take you for a man who liked being late."

"You killed him because we were late?" Seth questions. He lets a hint of humor ease into his tone, but his gun still sits at his side.

It's only then that Officer Walsh takes his gaze from me and focuses on Seth.

"No. I shot him because I don't need him and he knows too much."

"Good to know that's how you do business." Seth's criticism is rewarded with a tilt of Walsh's head.

"What's his name?" I question.

"It doesn't matter." Walsh looks between the two of us, making me second-guess his plan of action.

"It does to us," Seth speaks for me, and I don't mind in the least, since the same words were going to come out of my mouth. I want to know everything about the dead man lying on the floor. What he did, who he worked for, and most importantly: why he was standing beside Walsh in the first place?

"Joey Esposito."

"Anything else we should know about him?" Seth asks and Walsh simply stares at him. I didn't come here for a pissing contest.

"What do you want?" I speak loud and clearly, breaking up whatever's starting between the two of them.

"To share two things with you. Both of them are pieces of information I think you'll find valuable," he says and then nudges the leg of the dead man on the floor. It's a dull prod with no emotion behind it, just enough to be noticed. "He worked for Romano."

Just hearing the name *Romano* raises the small hairs on the back of my neck. I feel my eyes narrow but other than that, I keep my composure. Seth does the same. Remaining still, unmoving. Unbothered.

That's more like him.

"I'll hand over the whereabouts of Romano freely. I'd prefer for you…" he pauses to glance at Seth before adding, "the two of you, to know that I'm willing to negotiate."

"Handing something over for free isn't a part of

negotiations. Negotiations require something in return." Seth corrects him and I have to fight the grin that plays at my lips.

The irritation in Walsh's demeanor is something I didn't know I'd enjoy so much. Maybe because it's obvious he wanted the upper hand by killing this poor fuck the second we got here. Maybe it's because Seth isn't making it easy for Walsh. Either way, I make a mental note to tell him I like his style when he's not following.

Before Walsh can respond, I comment, "How'd you get the information regarding Romano's whereabouts? Esposito just gave it to you? Or did he think you had a deal?" I let the implication hang in the air, that his deals aren't to be trusted as I take a step forward.

"He came to me, wanting something I couldn't offer. He decided to rat, I decided to skip the judicial system and deliver his sentence to save some financial burdens. How's that sound? Reasonable, *Mr. Cross*? Besides, I already knew where Romano was. That's not the information Joey was giving me. Romano's in protective custody."

The way he says my name makes my skin crawl. He ignores the silent snarl and continues talking, grabbing the back of a simple metal chair, letting it drag across the floor with a shrill sound.

"What's more important is that the indictment was dropped." He leaves the chair in front of Seth, then grabs another. There's a stack of them, and he delivers one to each of us before taking a seat himself.

Seth hesitates, so I sit down first. Both of us, across from Walsh. All of us holding our guns, but settled in our laps.

"Dropped?" I question, feeling my curiosity, my disbelief even, show on my face.

"It's confidential."

"So he gave something up?" Seth surmises and Walsh shrugs but wears a slight grin. "Fucking rat."

"Jail or death. He didn't have many options, did he?" Walsh comments.

"He made a mistake coming back," Seth responds and then sits back in his seat when I give him a look.

"What's the other thing?" I ask Walsh, squaring my shoulders and moving away from the subject of Romano. "You said you had two things to say. The first is that you have Romano's whereabouts. What's the second? I'm guessing it's these recordings you say you have? Negotiation and blackmail in the same conversation?"

Walsh tosses a small notebook into my lap. It's small and something easily tucked away, like something that would fit inside of a wallet. "The hotel Romano's been placed in and his room number. He's got three police offers posted next door. If they hear banging around and screaming, they've been told to let it happen."

"And you're fine with that?" I question, feeling my shoulders tighten. "It's got 'setup' written all over it."

"I'm not letting Romano walk away. He's the reason Marcus came back here." Walsh leans forward, his elbows resting on his knees so he's closer to me as he tells us, "I want him dead but it can't be on our hands. Too many people are involved. Take him. I've read the files on Aria Talvery. I saw what happened with your brother."

"You saw what happened to Tyler?" I question him, not understanding how he knew.

"Tyler?" he responds with a shake of his head. "Carter. Carter is with Aria, unless I'm mistaken." It's silent for a long moment.

"What happened with Tyler?" he asks when the quiet air lingers for too long.

"Nothing of your concern." I shift my weight in my chair as Walsh leans back further. "I want Romano for an entirely different reason."

"Then take him. I'm giving him to you, both to start off with a good rapport."

"Seconds before blackmailing us?" Seth interrupts him and Officer Walsh shrugs. "Both to have a good rapport. And to show Marcus I'm here and I'm not going anywhere."

"Marcus came back… here? For Romano?" I question, thinking back nearly a decade ago when I first learned about the bogeyman that is Marcus. "How long have you been after him?"

"Six years now," Officer Walsh tells me and it doesn't add up. Marcus never left. Marcus couldn't have been in New York fucking with Walsh while keeping up his reputation down here and pulling strings. The cogs turn slowly as I assess Walsh, wondering where it went wrong, needing to know what piece is missing.

The reality of what Walsh is willing to do in order to get to Marcus coming into focus.

Seth readjusts in the seat, shifting his gun from hand to hand and then he stands, pushing the metal chair back as he does and stating, "I'd rather stand if you two don't mind."

I don't move my gaze from Walsh, who merely watches.

His pale blue eyes raise to mine and then to Seth's as he says, "My only request is that you don't kill him at the hotel. Make it look like he took off and skipped town. Do that and he's yours."

"In exchange for?" I wait for the other shoe to drop. Seth stands still to my left. His wrists are crossed in front of him and one hand still holds the gun.

"What do you think I want?" he asks lowly.

He's slow to pull a recorder out of his pocket, and with the click of a button, Seth's voice is heard and then the sound of something creaking. I recognize it immediately.

"Who's this fuck?" he asks and I answer, "Hal. The second he wakes up, bring him to the cellar."

"You have questions for him?" Seth asks.

"No. No questions."

Officer Walsh stops the recording, although the visual memory of opening the trunk and showing Seth in the parking lot behind The Red Room continues playing out in my mind.

"What was bugged?" I ask Walsh, running my thumb along the rim of the barrel. Motherfucker. Anger courses through me uncontained inside, although I don't let it show.

"I'm guessing a gift from Marcus?" Walsh speculates with a glimmer in his eye. "The recording has enough evidence for me to piece together how you got hold of Mr. Hal Brooks, that he was alive when you took him... and what you did to him after."

"What exactly are you implying?" A trace of anger can be heard in the hiss of my question.

"That you're fucked... unless you've got information for me. It was in his clothes and found on Mr. Brooks body."

It sinks in slowly. Marcus bugged Hal. He set me up. Between Marcus, Walsh and Romano, the list of men to kill keeps getting longer.

"What information are you looking for?" I ask, looking him dead in the eyes.

Walsh merely stands, glancing at the dead man on the floor and the dark pool of red that's staining his face as he looks off to the front double doors in the distance.

"I'll contact you when I have specifics." With that he stands, leaving me to calculate every possible way we can kill him. He's a man hell-bent on vengeance and willing to burn everything that lies between him and it.

As the two of us stand up slowly, watching his hands and how he places the gun back in his holster, Walsh adds, "Go tonight for Romano. Tomorrow the teams change. I mean it when I say I intend to have a good rapport with you two."

Turning his back to us, he places the chair he'd taken on top of the stack. "Unless you want to help me clean up, I think you'd better getting going."

The metal of the gun is warm when I slip it behind my back in the holster, taking in everything I can about Officer Cody Walsh. It's silent, save for the, "Until next time," Walsh gives us on our way out.

Neither of us speaks until we're far enough out in the distance.

Still seething, we both climb into the car and listen to the *thunk* of the doors closing as the sound of crickets off in the distance fades to silence.

"We're screwed if he mails the recordings or hands them out to the fucking FBI." Seth says the fucking obvious, tapping his foot in the car.

We should have incinerated him. That dead fuck and all the evidence along with it. Instead, I had to freak the fuck out over shit that happened years ago.

Seth keeps up with the tapping. Tap, tap, tapping as my frustration grows.

"Knock it the fuck off."

"I'm thinking," he retorts and then lets out a "fuck" and punches the side of the door.

"Feel better?" I ask him when he lifts his fist to examine his hand.

"Much," he answers dryly.

The keys jingle in the ignition as the engine turns over, humming to life. Seth rolls his window down, breathing in the cold air until he comes up with a solution

"I'll find out where the info is and get rid of it then get rid of him," he speaks.

"That easy?"

"If we put him in the cellar, yeah. That easy."

"You think he'll tell us where it is?" I glance at him and let out an uneasy exhale, shaking my head as the wind blows by. "I don't think he will. I think he'd die before quitting."

"Then how?"

"Declan has to find something."

"Declan's looking into something?"

"I asked him to look into something before I know whether or not it's a dead end. I don't know yet; it may be useless."

He's reluctant to nod, but he does. "And what about Romano?"

"Go tonight and take three men with you. Two for

lookouts." The order comes out as easy as the plan should be. "If he's in their custody, he's unarmed and it should be in and out."

"We'll hit him with chloroform. Keep it quiet."

"Just make sure you take out any cameras first. And stay silent, wear masks. Don't trust it not to be recorded."

"Got it. Want me to send a report to Carter first?" he asks and I stare off to the right side as the car comes to a stop. Just happens to be the graveyard. "No, I can do it. I'll tell him."

I'll tell my brother just how badly I've fucked up. With all of this.

Then I'll deal with Bethany.

And then Romano.

CHAPTER 13

Bethany

My eyes feel so dry but I can't keep them closed. Every time they shut, I see Jenny, in the hands of a villain. She's out there and I'm lying in a comfortable bed, protected and doing nothing.

The thin slit of light from the hallway that lays across the bedroom floor and hits the dresser widens as a soft creak fills the quiet room. Jase's footsteps are cautious and muted.

"You don't have to be quiet," I let him know although I have to clear my throat after. It's raw and in need of a hot cup of tea. A luxury I can afford, as I'm not *missing and presumed dead.*

"You're not sleeping?"

"How could I?" I answer Jase with the question as he

walks to the bed and lowers himself to sit by my side, making the mattress dip where my legs lay.

He tells me, "I didn't expect you in here."

For a moment, I reconsider every thought that brought me back to his bedroom and ask, "Do you want me to leave?" If he does, I will. If he doesn't, I'll stay. Simply because I want to be here. I still want to be next to him when I do fall asleep. I want him to hold me, but I'm too prideful to ask. More than that, I'm ashamed that after all the lies, I still feel like I need him.

His answer is quick. "Never."

"I don't want to give you an ultimatum." I spit out the words that I've been saying over and over in my head the last hour or so. "I hate them and I think they're awful."

Jase is deadly silent, listening to what I have to say. I can feel his eyes on me although I don't look up at him. Resting his head on my thigh that's covered by the blanket, he waits for me to continue.

"It hurts to even say it. I can't deal with lies. I don't want to be a woman who lets a man lie to her."

"I won't."

"I don't know that I believe you." Finally looking into his eyes, I suck in a deep inhale to calm my words. "I can't stay if I find out you've lied to me about something. I can't be with you if that's all there is between us."

"There's nothing else and there will never be anything else."

My mother used to warn us about 'always' and 'nevers.' Especially about the people who speak them with certainty.

With the window cracked, a gust of cool air blows

in trailing along my skin and with it, the ends of my hair tickle down my bare arm as I prop myself up. "You sound so sure."

"I am." His hard jaw seems sharper in the faint light with the shadows from the moon. There's an intensity that swirls in his eyes, but it seems different now. Not so much riddled with fear as it is with loss and regret.

Or maybe it's a reflection of myself, maybe it's just what I want to see. He may be certain, but I'm not so sure of anything anymore.

I can only nod, and lie back down. Back to his bed although I'm on my side and I intend to sleep all night with my back to him. I'll do it every night until the hurt goes away. That deep pain that's settled into my chest like fucking cancer.

"Is there anything else I can..." Jase pauses and I hear him readjust as the bed jostles.

"Anything else you can say or do?" I finish the question for him, my eyes open and staring straight ahead at nothing in particular.

"Is there?" he asks when I don't answer the question I raised.

"We just move on, don't we?" I tell him, feeling that pain spread like a web, tiny and sticking to everything inside of me as it spins. "That's what happens."

"Why do you sound so defeated?"

"Because it hurts, it all hurts and I don't know how to fix it other than to believe you. Even that hurts right now."

The mattress groans as he leans forward, rubbing my back as I lie there, refusing to give in to anger. "What matters is that Jenny's alive." My bottom lip trembles and my throat goes tight as I ask, "You're going to save her, right? You're going to bring her home?"

"I'm doing everything I can," Jase whispers as he lies down next to me although he's not under the covers. He pulls me in closer to him and as much as I'd love to shove him away for everything he's done, I need to be held by this man for the very same reasons.

"When we were little, she was my hero," I admit to Jase, still staring ahead at the blank wall that's been a photo album to me all night, flicking through memory after memory. "I was thinking about the time when I'd just reached high school and how she helped me with my English homework. She loved poetry. She was so good at it."

It sounds like Jase is going to say something, but instead he stays quiet. He kisses me on my shoulder though, through the sleepshirt and then on my jaw by my ear. The kind of kiss where I'm forced to close my eyes. When he lays my arm in the dip at my side and then rests his forearm in front of me, I twine my fingers with his.

His touch means more to me right now than I think he'll ever know.

The second I part my lips to thank him, he speaks first. "Tell me more about her."

"I don't know what to tell you. She was my big sister, the one who looked out for me, helping me with everything... until it all went wrong."

"What went wrong?"

"Our mom did. That's when everything changed." The hollowness in my chest seems to grow thinking about it all, so I stay quiet. The silence doesn't stretch for long.

"Do you still hate me?"

For lying about my sister while I was mourning her?
For lying about scaring me into staying with you?
For lying about the debt and taking advantage of me?

The questions line themselves up in my head, but stay unspoken.

"No," I answer him. "I hate what you did, but I don't hate you."

"Why do I feel like things aren't okay?" he questions and that gets a reaction from me. Fighting the covers with my legs, I turn around to face him, propping myself up with my elbow and feeling the comforter fall down my shoulder.

"Because I'm still upset," I say and frustration comes out in my tone. "What would you have me do, Jase?" The exasperated question escapes easily from my lips. "I don't know if you've lied about something else... or if you will."

"There are no other lies." Anger colors his statement and reflects in his gaze.

"I don't believe you." There's no emotion in my words, only facts. "There are only so many times you can lie to a person. Only so many. But what am I really going to do? That's why I'm hurt. I don't want to leave you." Fuck, saying the words makes me feel weak, down to my core. I don't want to leave him. Not just for my sister's sake, either. "I feel *pathetic*." I practically spit the word out.

"Do you forgive me?"

"You said you were sorry." That's all I can say.

"That doesn't answer my question."

"It doesn't matter," I tell him.

"It does."

"I forgave you without you even apologizing. It's about

trusting you and trusting myself after falling for you. The trust isn't there anymore," I admit.

"I can give you reasons to trust me--"

"Time will," I cut him off. "Even when I hate you, you're still what I need. You don't understand how much I feel that I need you."

"I do. I know what that's like," he confides in me and I feel like it's the truth. Why else would he want me here? Why else would a man like him deal with me, in this state, right now?

When I don't respond, he asks me, "How can I make it right?"

"You can start with finding Jenny and bringing her home."

"I can't guarantee--" he starts to say, but I don't want to hear it.

"I finally let go... I let go and she was still out there." My voice cracks. If I had kept looking, if I'd kept asking around and demanding answers... Maybe she would be home now.

"I can't make that promise to you, Bethany."

Letting go of the regret, I focus on what we can do now when I tell him, "I know you can't promise, but I wish you could."

Instead of lying down like I think he's going to do, he sits up and walks his way around the bed to stand in front of me. "I have to go," he tells me and I nod into the pillow, keeping my hands down on the bed, although I question if I should reach up and wrap them around his neck to pull him down for a kiss. Is it so bad that I want to be kissed when I'm hurting? Even if it's by the one who caused the pain?

"Where are you going?" I ask him, not hiding the surprise or the slight worry in my cadence as I glance at the clock. "It's late." I say the excuse as I sit up and wrap my arms around myself.

I expect him to hesitate, to lie or to give some vague response. "I'm going to kill the man who murdered my brother," he answers and my heart lurches inside of me. All the pain I've been going through and turmoil, he may have had a hand in it, but I forgot he suffers through it too.

"Jase, are you okay?" I don't think I've ever pushed myself up quicker in bed as I get onto my knees and move toward him.

"I'm fine, anxious though," he answers me as I sit in front of him, neither of us touching each other in the dark night. It's all shadows and cool gusts of air between us and I wish it would go away; I wish I could change everything.

"I'm sorry," I whisper, and do exactly what I wanted to do a moment ago for myself, but right now it's for him. Sitting up taller, I press my lips to his for a tender kiss, my fingers brushing against his stubble and then laying across the back of his neck. Jase tilts his head down and cupping the back of my head, keeps me there for a second longer. Just one more beat.

"Are you going to be all right?" I ask him in a whisper, my lips close to his, not wanting to let go.

"I'll be fine," he answers me and I don't think he's lying. I think that *he* thinks he really will be fine, in a situation where nothing at all is fine.

"Do you care that I'm going to kill him?" He doesn't let me go as he asks the question.

"Only in the sense that I care about what it does to

you." The answer is immediate and true to the core. Maybe it's wrong, but there's so much that's not right that I simply don't care about being wrong anymore.

"I want you with me. You can know, or you can guess, you can ignore it all. I don't care so long as you're with me."

"I want to know," I tell him even though a tremor of fear runs through me.

"All I care about is you being here when I get back. Tell me you'll be here."

"I'll be here."

I wish I'd told him I loved him, but he kisses me and then leaves me breathless on the bed. I can feel it in his kiss and when he leaves, when the door is closed and he's long gone, I ask as though he's still here with me, *why won't you tell me you love me?*

I refuse to believe it's not love. It's fucked up a million ways and then some, but this is love.

CHAPTER 14

Jase

"IN SOME CULTURES, PEOPLE BURY THE MEN they murder face down so they can't come back to haunt them."

Four stories up in the vacant and grand estate, the large windows are open and the rooms are all bare. The empty old office is bigger than the entire house I grew up in. The ceilings are tall; the light wood floors shine with polish. When Romano left his place weeks ago, he took off and got rid of everything. One day he was here, the next he was gone. The worst decision he made was coming back.

"Face down? Like in their grave?" Seth asks from across the large room. There aren't any lights in the room; the full moon and the streetlights give us everything we need. He's still dressed in jeans and a shirt, both black.

His men are downstairs sweeping the place and preparing for what's to come, while we're up here with our guest of honor.

I nod, listening to the muffled noises that come from behind the balled-up rag in Romano's mouth. Hysteria is setting in for the old man as his face turns red and Carter, Declan and Daniel join us. He's never looked so old to me. So close to a fucking heart attack and then death. Wouldn't that be ironic? If the fucker had a heart attack while tied down in that desk chair and we didn't even get a chance to kill him.

"They thought if they buried the men they killed face down, when their spirits woke up, they'd be disoriented," I explain to Seth and to whoever else is listening.

Seth lets out a rough chuckle, playing with a knife as he sits in a wingback chair in the corner. The leather is old and cracked. I guess that's why Romano left it behind. Everything left in the room was meant to be thrown away. Now Romano's been added to that category.

"I've heard of feeding the dead to pigs. They'll eat anything," Seth answers.

"Can't bury a man if he dies with dynamite in his lap, can you? Or feed what's left of him to the pigs?" Carter questions and then pats my shoulder as he enters the room. He only glances at Romano, not paying him much mind as he walks around the room. This estate has to be a hundred years old. It was a family legacy. One that's ending tonight.

Although the conversation borders on lighthearted in tone, tension is thick in the room.

"This used to be your office?" Carter asks Romano as he leans forward, placing a hand on the soon-to-be dead man's shoulder. From behind the rag comes nothing but rage and the muted sounds of what I assume are curse words.

I wonder what it's like to be him right now. I'd rather have a heart attack than to be him right now.

Carter only smirks at him, standing up and pushing off of his shoulder, sending Romano rolling away in the wheeled desk chair. Gagged and tied down, this is how he'll die. In the room where he made all of his decisions. Decisions to murder and decisions that require consequences.

"Any situations tonight?" Carter asks Seth who shakes his head. "In and out, he was sleeping so the chloroform was easy. Overall it was," he says as he looks Carter in the eyes, "uneventful."

"And the detail in the next room? Did they try to interfere?"

Seth answers, "Didn't see them, didn't hear them. It was all over in under ten minutes. Even if it was filmed, we were masked and didn't talk. There's no way to ID us."

"Good work," I chime in and my brother agrees.

"Explosives are planted everywhere but the main room where we hid the cash in the safe. It'll look like he came back to hide evidence, but mistakenly set it off too soon," Carter explains.

"What a tragedy." Daniel's comment drips with sarcasm. Out of all of us he's been the most quiet, the most still. Leaning against the back wall and staring at Romano all night.

Romano says something. It could be his last words for all I care, they won't be heard.

Declan adds, "It keeps the feds off our back, they go away. I want them the fuck out of here. And we take over the upper east side."

"All our problems solved." Triumph comes darkly from Carter's voice.

Almost all. Marcus and Walsh are becoming more difficult problems by the day, but I keep that opinion to myself.

"I wish they all knew," Daniel speaks up. As he kicks off the wall and walks closer to the far edge of the room to look down at the tied-up man, the light sends shadows over the harsh expression on his face. "It's too quick and not public enough for what you deserve," he tells Romano. His voice is hoarse, and anger and mourning both linger there.

The memory of Tyler dead in the street plays tricks on my mind as I look out the large window feeling the cool breeze against my face. The cast iron fence separates the estate from the road and it's just beneath us. The road ahead is a backroad; many don't travel on it and it's not the road Tyler where died, but any black road slick with rain will carry that memory forever.

"Justice is a funny thing, isn't it?" I murmur as I tap my blunt nails along the windowsill, opening the window even more, as much as I can to feel the cold air blow in. "It never feels like enough."

"What?" Daniel asks from behind me, so I turn around to face him.

"It's never going to feel like enough… because it's never going to be all right." With the singular truth exposed, a raw pain grows from my empty lungs and radiates upward.

"I'm grateful he didn't get away and the feds didn't fuck this up for us. We'll spread it around, that we didn't like him talking to the cops," Carter says and looks pointedly at Seth, who nods. Rumors travel fast in this town and everyone needs to know it was us. Romano fucked with us. Now he's dead. That'll make a lot of other pricks question whether or not they're willing to do the same.

"What about Tyler?" Daniel asks. His forehead creases as he continues, "They should know Romano killed him and that's what gave him a death sentence."

"We'd be admitting we didn't know the truth until recently," Carter speaks up, shaking his head. "It's easier to keep it a secret."

A lie, hisses in my ear, and I have to turn away from my brothers, once again looking out into the empty street only to see the ghost of memories there.

"I don't like it." Daniel disagrees with Carter. Seth and Declan are quiet, simply observing the two of them.

"Tyler deserves justice," I speak up before being conscious of it. "It shouldn't be kept a secret."

"Romano dies tonight." Carter's harsh words whip through the air. "What more do you want?"

I'm surprised by Daniel's words as he says, "Humiliation, pain… I want it to be a spectacle." He's still filled with hate over Tyler's death. He's still angry. He's still grieving. I'm convinced the five stages of grieving aren't like steps where you take one after the other. I think they're waves that constantly crash onto the shore and you never know which one will hit you.

"That's not going to help our FBI situation," Declan answers, peeking up from the corner of the room where he's standing behind Seth. I can feel all their eyes on me, but I don't look back yet. All I can look at are the spikes that line the top of his iron fence. All I can think about is how awful it would be to die like that, to fall onto the spiked fence beneath us and be impaled next to an asphalt road. It'd be the last thing he ever looked at.

"We decided this was how it would be... now you want to wait?" Carter questions, his voice tight with incredulity.

"No, we don't have to wait." I turn to finish my thought, looking at Daniel as I suggest, "We can throw him out this window. That would be a *spectacle*, as you called it."

Daniel smirks while Declan lets out a chuckle and then asks, "Wait, are you serious?"

"He can die committing suicide by jumping onto a spiked fence," Daniel says and smiles over Romano's muffled pleas. The man's fighting in his chair now, causing it to roll slightly across the floor. I kick the back of it gently, just to push him away from me and torture him some more.

"Who would kill themselves that way?" Declan asks. "Who commits suicide by spearing himself onto a fence?"

"No one," I answer him and Daniel adds, "That's the point."

"That would send a message," Seth comments although it's not meant to agree or disagree. He stays neutral in all of this.

Carter's voice is low as he says, "It would send a message to the feds too. That we don't care they're here and that we're still running this town. Is that the message you want to send?"

"That's the message we *need* to send," Daniel presses. "What are they going to do? We don't leave evidence. They'll know, but they can't do anything about it."

"Just like they can't do anything about Tyler," I say and my statement is the nail in the coffin for me. Romano murdered our brother and left him on the street to die. "This is justice."

He'll do the same.

"No one knew about Tyler; how could they have done anything?" That's the problem, isn't it? With so many lies and secrets, no one could do anything for Tyler. It was just a tragedy.

Just like Jenny. I think about how many times Bethany went to the cops and filed a missing persons report for her sister. How they told her they were sorry, and they didn't know what happened when the trunk was found.

"We need to do this, Carter," I say and look him dead in the eyes, feeling a numbing prick flow over my skin. "No accident, no dynamite. We give him the death he earned."

Time ticks slowly, with Seth shifting behind me and Declan staring at Daniel, who's waiting for Carter's final decision. *Tick, tick, tick.* It's too slow.

"Take the cash, leave the safe empty and open. Wipe for prints." Carter gives the order and I walk from the open window to Daniel, feeling the cold gust of wind at my back carrying Romano's muffled screams.

"You all right?" I ask him lowly so it's just between the two of us, and he nods although he can't look me in the eyes, he can't look away from Romano.

"Who gets to do it?" he asks me although his voice is coarse and he has to clear it. "Who gets to do the honors?"

"You can if you want." I give it to him. I'll suffer the rest of my life, hating that Tyler died in my place. Whether Romano breathes again, whether I kill him, none of it will change that. But at least now everyone will know. And that's something.

"It was supposed to be you," he reminds me, as if there's any way I could forget.

"I know, but doing this isn't going to bring Tyler back." Daniel's expression wavers, the hardness falls for a moment and he nods again. I watch as the cords in his neck tense.

"If we're doing this, it has to be done clean," Declan speaks up. I'm not sure if he disagrees and thinks we should go the safe route, or if he's simply covering our bases.

"We're always clean," Seth answers him.

"Let the feds see," I tell Declan. "Let everyone know." I pat Daniel on the back and then look Carter in the eyes as I say, "No one takes from us and gets away with it."

"It's settled then," Carter agrees. "And the men that came back with him? What about them?"

"Make it clean," Declan repeats to Carter, the undertone of his voice harsh. Romano's cries can still be heard and I kick the chair just slightly, sending him rolling backward again.

"There's no deal to offer any of Romano's men, no loose ends," Seth says and nods.

I wait until Seth lifts his eyes to mine. "Go through every part of this town. Every asshole who ever got a paycheck from him. Find them in their homes, at the bar. I don't care if they're balls deep in the back room of a strip joint. Find them, kill them."

"They die tonight," Carter talks as he walks to where

I was, no doubt judging what it'll take to make sure Romano's impaled. It won't take much at all. It's just outside the window. "There aren't many left. We already have locations on most of them."

"They'll scatter like roaches if we wait until tomorrow and the FBI doesn't know yet, but the moment they find Romano, they'll be everywhere. So we end it tonight," Daniel agrees, walking to Romano and turning the chair. He has to crouch down to be at his eye level. "Wipe them all out."

"Start with him," I speak to Daniel, and he looks over his shoulder at me. His lips are pressed in a straight line, with a grim look covering his face.

"End it," I tell him. Carter steps to the side, and we all wait.

Pushing the gagged, screaming man with a bright red face to the window, Daniel looks out onto the road—a backroad that will be empty until the morning.

The gag comes off first, bringing a stream of Italian profanity from the dried throat of this dead fuck. Romano pulls on the ropes, fighting as best he can against them. It's foolish really, he should wait until we untie him for his best chance, but he doesn't, knowing his end is coming.

Seth's the one to cut the rope at his feet; one quick swipe and the nylon threads are released. Romano attempts to run, still bound to the back of the heavy leather chair and he falls hard on his side, seething in pain. The crack of his skull hitting the floor ricochets in the room.

With Carter holding his left side and me holding his right, Seth cuts the binds and helps us hold him up, holding him steady and restraining him as he tries to run and fight. I can't breathe. My muscles are too coiled as Romano struggles with the last bit of strength he has left in him.

Backing him up to the window, I stare at Daniel's face. I expect anger, I expect hate, but agony is all that's on his face. It's still not enough; being the one to end Romano… it's not enough. It won't bring Tyler back.

We release our hold as Romano falls backward from the force of the shove Daniel gives him in his chest. Romano's arms whip out to grab onto whatever he can, but there's nothing there, nothing that can keep him upright. His scream dulls as he falls the four stories and then it's silenced.

Staring down at him and the scene, I no longer see Tyler. The street's empty. All I see is a man who killed all his life, a man impaled with the life draining from him slowly.

Turning to Seth, I tell him, "Check that he's dead, then find the rest."

CHAPTER 15

Bethany

IT'S BEEN QUIET THE LAST FEW DAYS. TOO QUIET.

The ominous feeling that settles in when you know things won't last... that's in the air. I've been breathing it in and suffocating from it. Jase is being careful with me and both of us are feeling bad for the other one.

It's easy to give someone sympathy, it's easy to love them. Accepting their love though, accepting it in the way they're able to give... that's the difficult part, because that's where you get hurt.

I forgive him, but I'm waiting for the next bad thing to happen.

Jase is just waiting, on edge and waiting for something... I don't know what.

The other end of the line goes to voicemail. So I dial

non-office is now my hideaway. The smell of old books and leather is too much to resist.

Ring. Ring.

On the second ring, it picks up and I recognize the voice instantly.

"Laura," I say and my gut falls. I wasn't expecting her to answer. "I didn't know you were working day shifts this week."

Animosity and betrayal stir in my stomach. More than that though, I miss her.

"Bethany?" She sounds surprised to hear my voice.

"I just wanted to call about Michelle, the pregnant patient with pica on floor two, and maybe talk to Aiden…" I trail off, waiting for Laura to tell me she'll get him. After a few seconds of silence and then the way she says my name, I know that's not going to happen.

"Bethany," she says but I can already tell there's too much sympathy in her tone. "Michelle died two days ago. I'm sorry. I thought Aiden called."

The leather turns hot under my tight grip. I can barely breathe. When I worked in pediatrics before this for my internship, death was common. It was so common I'd check the paper for the obituaries before coming into work so I'd be prepared. It's also why I left. At the center, it rarely happens, but now it feels like death's following me everywhere.

"Beth? Are you there?"

"I'm here," I answer her although my body's still tense and it hurts to swallow.

"You weren't answering my texts and I know you're mad, but I thought you knew. I swear. I'm so sorry."

"How did it happen?"

"Magnets. They obstructed her bowels," Laura answers.

"If I'd been working--"

"Don't think like that."

"I had a rapport with her." I can't even say her name as tears prick my eyes. She was young and beautiful. Before getting pregnant, she was healthy. If only, if only. I think it too much now. Every day I wonder 'what if' in all aspects of my life. It's not a healthy way to live.

"She wasn't well and..." Laura stops when she hears my quick inhale. I'm not crying, but I'm damn close to it.

"There was nothing any of us could have done. The behavioral approach was working and she was released. Her husband checked her out... it happened in her home."

With a hand over my heated face, I focus on calming down, but it takes a long moment. Struggling not to lose it, I debate on simply hanging up.

"I'm sorry," Laura tells me again and I don't know what to reply. It's not okay, but that's the answer we're supposed to give, isn't it? That or thank you, but there's nothing to be thankful for right now.

"You need to come back to work," Laura tells me when the silence stretches.

"Everything's changed."

My voice is tight when I answer her. "I want to come back." Focusing on breathing, I try to calm down. "I can't believe she's dead. It feels like I was just with her."

"Tragedy happens." Seconds pass as I try to accept it, staring at the unlit fireplace.

"You should come back." I'm grateful for Laura's distraction as she adds, "Aiden's gone for three days and he told me to schedule you for next week. So you're on."

My eyes lift to the bookshelves, feeling wider, more alert. "I can come back to work?"

"We need you. There's so much that's happened."

The way she says it makes my heart still and I can feel a deep crease settle between my brow as I ask, "What? What happened?"

"I can't tell you over the phone; just start back on Monday."

A cold prick flows over my skin, knowing something's wrong, but not knowing what. "Okay." I take a moment, which feels awkward and tense, but I make sure Laura knows I'm genuine when I tell her, "Thank you."

"Are we okay?" she asks me softly. I can practically see her nervously wrapping her finger around the phone cord in the office like she does. It's a habit I picked up from her.

I answer her honestly, "I don't understand why you did it. Why you called him and didn't tell me."

"There's a lot you don't know."

"You could tell me," I offer her. "Really, if you'd told me no, or if you told me you called him before he showed up…"

"I… I can't tell you right now, but soon? I can tell you soon, if you want."

"I want to know. I do."

"And then we'll be okay?" she asks me as if that's all she wants.

"Yeah," I answer her even though I don't know if it's truthful. I don't know why so many people are hiding secrets. Or why each one hurts more than the last.

When I hang up the phone with her, I hear the front door close from all the way down the long hall. Jase is home and it surprises me how much I want to go to him, how much I want him to hold me like he does every time he gets back and just before he leaves.

I wait for him, holding my breath at first, but I can't hear where he's going or what he's doing. Leaving my phone on the glass table, I pick my book back up, although my gaze flicks to the open door.

CHAPTER 16

Bethany

H E'S BEEN QUIET, BUT THERE'S A LOOK IN HIS eyes that's anything but. I can feel the tension crackle and it promises that if I follow him, I'll be given everything I could possibly want in this moment. And so I do. The second he looks at me, I close my book and leave it there to go to him.

"Come on," he commands but it's soft and low, pleading almost. My heart yearns to follow him quickly; to show him I accept his demands.

"I don't want this distance between us anymore." Jase's voice is calming and deep.

"I don't either," I admit to him and reach out to take his hand when he offers it. There's something about the roughness along his knuckles and the warmth of his skin that's soothing. His touch consoles a part of me that's desperate to heal.

"Trust works both ways," Jase tells me as I gauge the changes in the fire room. Everything's been moved out, most notably the chaise and the wooden bench. In place of the plush white rug is a black blanket, large and heavy. The room's barren, but still beautiful, with the crystal fireplace and lit chandeliers.

"Both ways," I repeat, registering his words and wondering what he has planned.

He said he found a solution to our problem. Funny how a man's solution involves sex... or so I assume. To be honest though, I need this.

I need *him* like this. I close my eyes knowing *we* need this.

"Strip here." He gives me orders as he places a handful of things in the middle of the blanket.

A candle, a lighter, a bottle of ethanol, some sort of white cloth, and the weighted blanket. Tremors of pleasure send a warmth flowing through me, meeting at my core and heating instantly.

By the time I've stripped to nothing, he's done the same. The light from the fire emphasizes every etched muscle in his taut skin. His cock is already rigid and my bottom lip drops at the thought of being at this man's mercy.

A deep, rough chuckle whips my eyes from his length to his gaze. "Ever needy and greedy, aren't you?" he teases me and that's when I see the glimmer of light that reflects off the blade. The tension rises, stifling me, wrapping its way around me... and I love it. I crave it. It does nothing but ignite a fire inside of me.

My feet patter on the slick black blanket beneath us

as I make my way to him, tucking my hair behind my ear as I prepare to drop to my knees in front of him. I want to please him, to prove to him that I still desire him, that there's still a roaring fire between us. I don't get a chance to though.

Catching my elbow, Jase stops me and instead puts his hand on mine, pulling my fingers back and making me hold my hand out flat. He's silent as he gives me the knife.

"It's heavy," I comment weakly as he sits cross-legged and I do the same in front of him. The heat from the fire is the only thing that keeps the chills of the cool air away. My heart races as I glance at the small silvery scar still on his chest.

"I want us both to play," he tells me, wrapping my hand around the handle of the blade and then bringing it to his chest. "First you need to shave me."

The command is simple although my gaze shifts from the small smattering of hair on his chest to his eyes. Scooting closer to him, I watch the way his throat dips, the way the cords tighten as I prepare for the first stroke.

Before I can press the blade to his skin, he lays a hand on each of my hips, holding me steady. The warmth of the fire is nothing compared to his touch. With every small exhale, I drag the blade down carefully, feeling it nick each hair along his chest. Breathing in, I then drag the blade over his skin, blowing softly across it as I go and gently bring the back of my fingers across his body to check on the smoothness of it.

"Don't leave any behind," he tells me, sitting upright and still not moving.

"Does it hurt at all?" I ask him, running my fingers

over what I've just done and then moving the blade to a patch of fuzz on his upper pec by his shoulder.

"You're only shaving me," he answers with a handsome grin, mocking me.

"I mean the scar. Where I cut you before," I whisper, not looking into his eyes and then grabbing the cloth next to Jase to wipe the blade clean.

"No," he answers and then takes the knife from me. "It feels like a memory that fate made happen."

He does the same to me, shaving away the little bits of hair, making sure there's nothing between us that the fire would catch.

"You first," he tells me and he tips the bottle of ethanol, the cloth pressed against the opening. The smell of alcohol hits me as he wets the rag. "Where you put it, the fire will catch, but do it quickly." Before relaxing his shoulders and sitting back, he lights the candle. "Use this for the flame but hold it upright to keep the wax from dripping."

I've paid attention and I've seen what he does. Nodding, I know exactly what he's said and why it works, but still I hesitate, holding the rag in my hand and staring at his chest.

"What if I hurt you?"

"The blanket's fireproof and I can lie down, Bethany. I'm here, and you're more than capable."

I remember what it's like, the memory of the fire tickling then blazing. Heating my skin before vanishing and leaving me breathless and hungry for more. I can give that to him. The very idea of it makes me eager to do it.

Reaching out, I wipe the damp cloth against his skin in a small motion, not covering much area at all. My pulse is fast and my hand trembles slightly. I can't help it; the only thing that keeps me composed is the intimacy of the moment and his touch steadying me.

"A cross?" he questions and I let my lips kick up as I pick up the candle. "Over your heart," I answer him in a whisper as I lift the flame. It catches quicker than I anticipate, blazing in a short burst and vanishing as my heart races.

Releasing my shock in a single breath I look to Jase whose eyes are wide with desire as his chest rises higher. "Again," he commands in a deep groan. This time when I get closer to him, he grips my wrist holding the cloth out and tells me, "Use more and in a different spot. When it lights, press your body against mine and feel the aftershocks of the fire."

He takes his time, moving my hair behind me and telling me to braid it and be careful. Playing with fire is something we've always been warned not to do, and maybe that's why it's so exciting.

I do as he says, wondering what type of pleasure or pain it'll bring. I'm too slow the first time, too slow to feel anything but the heat of his chest where the reddened skin felt the kiss of fire. Still, with my body pressed against his and feeling the rumble of desire against his chest, it's erotic, it's forbidden and I want more of it.

"Fire needs fuel to stay alive. It has to breathe, but you can smother it. It needs to move, but you can deny it." His words are mesmerizing, and the feel of dulled flames extinguished as I press my body against his is unlike anything I've felt before. It's gone too fast.

Taking my hand, he runs the rag over my breasts

before I can run it down his body. I light him first and as I lean, the fire catches against my skin. As my head falls back, Jase presses his body to mine, gripping the hair at the base of my skull and pulling it back as his teeth scrape against my neck.

He takes control then, laying me down and playing with me, toying with the fire between us.

It's a dangerous game to play with fire, but I feel like he's made the rules. I feel invincible with him, like nothing matters except for what he tells me in that moment.

The light flicks between us, burning hot and roaring until it extinguishes. It happens so fast, but each moment seems more and more intense. Hotter, heavier and upping the stakes of how much of our skin is sensitized.

Until the lights have gone out and the heat dissipates, leaving me yearning for more.

More than the fire this time. I need *him*. The pieces of him that fire can't give me. I breathe into Jase's kiss, "I want you."

He devours me, pushing me to the floor and bracing himself above me, settling between my spread legs before tilting my hips how he wants them. Jase isn't gentle when he enters me. He teases me at first, pressing the head of his cock against my folds and sliding it up to my clit, rubbing me and taunting me before slamming inside of me to the hilt and making me scream. I watch him hold his breath as he does it, and he watches me just the same.

I'm lost in the lust of his gaze, lost in the gentle touches of his hands on my breasts where the fire just was as he pistons his hips, deliberately and with a steady pace that drives me to near insanity. He's controlled and measured, even through the intense pleasure. I feel him hit my back wall, the ridges of his cock pressing against every sensitive bundle of nerves as he fucks me like this. Deep and ruthlessly, but making every thrust push me higher.

I barely notice when he raises his body from mine. The heat from the fireplace blazes, but it doesn't compare to what it feels like to have his body on top of mine. I lift my shoulders off the ground, reaching up to hold on to his, but he shoves himself deep inside of me, making my back bow. Throwing my head back with pleasure, I see the lit candle, I see him tilt it to its side where it rolls away, the flame still lit, the fire growing, catching in a crevice of the hard wood floors.

Lighting ablaze.

"Jase!" I scream, pausing my body, but he doesn't stop, he crashes his lips to mine, hushing me as the fire roars behind us. Pressing my palms against him, I try to push him away so he can see, but he resists.

He ignores me to the point where I feel as though I've imagined it.

"Fire." I breathe out the word in a ragged whisper as he fucks me while the pleasure mounts and stirs in my belly; it overrides the fear. Jase tells me at the shell of my ear, "I know."

My heart races chaotically as I look into his eyes and he speaks with his lips close to mine, "Trust me." The fire behind us echoes in his eyes.

It takes me a moment to realize he's still. He's stopped. And the fire is real.

With the flames reflecting in his dark gaze, I reach up and pull him toward me, urging him on before kissing him.

The flames grow brighter and I can't stop watching them. Even as he ruts between my legs, bringing my pleasure higher and higher, my body getting hotter and the intensity of everything mixing with the fear and pain and utter rapture.

"It's on fire," I say and the fear creeps into my voice. "The room's on fire." Even so, Jase doesn't stop. He's savage as he fucks me into the ground, kissing his way down my neck. My nails dig into his skin as I hear and feel the fire grow. My heart pounds against his. "Trust me," he whispers.

The flames rise higher and higher, igniting against everything around us, even though it doesn't travel across the black blanket. "Kiss me," Jase commands, gripping my chin and pulling me back to him.

"Jase," I gasp his name, the fear and heat of the fire stealing me from him. His lips crash against mine and with a hand on my back and another on my ass, he moves me to the floor, pinning me there with his weight.

Thrusting himself inside of me, my back arches, my head falls back and I stare at the flickers of red and yellow flames as they engulf the room surrounding us.

And then, just in the moment when I'm breathless with fear, water rains down upon us. It comes down heavily. No sirens, no noises at all. Only water, leaving a chill from the cold droplets to bring goosebumps along my heated skin.

"There's always something to calm the fire," he groans in the crook of my neck and then drags his teeth along my throat as the deluge descends around us, extinguishing the flames. Every thrust is that much deeper as I lift my hips and dig my heels into his ass.

Even knowing it's safe, knowing the fire's gone, my heart still pounds with a primal instinct to run. I can't though, pinned beneath Jase and wanting more of him.

The light goes out around us, the flames diminished to nothing. The warmth of the room vanishes as the water washes us of the fear from being consumed by the fire.

Lifting his head up to look down at me, I stare into Jase's eyes as he presses himself deeper inside of me and then pulls out slowly, just to do it all again. Every agonizingly slow movement draws out my pleasure, raising the threshold and I whimper each time.

That's how I fall. Staring into his eyes longingly, praying for mercy to end it just as I whimper and beg him for more. Clinging to him as he hovers over me and loving this man. Loving him for all he is and knowing what I do. Knowing I never want to stop.

CHAPTER 17

Jase

"I LOVE THE SMELL AFTERWARD," I COMMENT, listening to the crackling of the flames in the fireplace. I lit it for the heat and the light both as Bethany lays against me, still on the floor.

Although I used the thick blanket to dry her off, her hair's still damp and the light from the fire casts shadows against her features, making me want to kiss along every vulnerable curve she has.

"The char?" she asks weakly, sleep pulling her in. The adrenaline should be waning now. Sleep will come for her soon and I hope it comes for me too.

"The water. It has a smell to it, when it puts out the fire."

"It does," she agrees and then lifts her head, placing a small hand on my chest as I stay on my back. "Will you tell me something?"

"What?"

"Anything," she requests in a single breath and lies against my chest. Spearing my fingers through her hair, I think of the worst of times in this room. I think of the fire, the way it feels like everything will end, the intensity and the simplicity of it all being washed away.

"Do you know how many men I've killed?" I ask her as the question rocks in my mind. "Because I don't."

Although I keep running my fingers along her back and then up to her neck, noting the way the fire warms her skin with a gorgeous glow, her own hand has stilled, and her breathing has stopped.

"Are you scared?" I ask her and she shakes her head, letting her hair tickle up my side. "I just don't want to do anything to stop you from saying more. I want to know."

"I used to keep count and memorize their names," I admit to her and remember when I first built this room. Its purpose was different then and the memory causes my throat to tighten.

"I'd sit here, and let the fire go. I'd let it burn whatever I'd brought, I'd let it spread and surround me. All the while, spouting off each person's name. Every person I murdered with intent or for survival. Every one of them. And there were many.

"At first, I'd give both first and last names. Then it became only first names because I'd run out of time otherwise. I thought if I could say them all before the fire went out, it'd be some kind of redemption. In the beginning I could do it. I could say them all before the water would come down. It never made me feel any better, but I did it anyway.

A SINGLE TOUCH

"Then I started forgetting," I confess. "Too many to remember, and the names all ran together. Some names I didn't want to say out loud. Names of men who I'll see in hell and smile knowing I put them there."

"Don't talk like that," Bethany admonishes me. She whispers, "I don't like you talking like that."

"Like what?"

"Like you're going to die and go to hell. Don't say that." The seriousness of her tone makes me smirk at her with disbelief.

"Of everything I've done and said, that's why you're scolding me?"

"I'm serious. I don't like it." She settles herself back down and nestles into me, seeming more awake now than before and with tears in her eyes.

"Why are you crying?"

"I'm not," she tells me. "And you're not a bad man. You just do bad things and there's a difference. God knows there's a difference, and I do too."

"Don't cry for me." I offer her a weak smile and brush under her eyes. Her soft skin begs me to keep touching her, to keep soothing her and never stop.

"I'm not," she repeats although she wipes her eyes and tries to hide it. "Don't talk about you dying... and we have a deal."

She doesn't look me in the eyes until I tilt her chin up, lifting my shoulders off the ground to kiss her gently and whisper, "deal," against her lips. I can feel her heart beat against mine. This is the moment I want to keep forever. If ever given a choice, I'll choose this one.

"Tell me something else." She states it like it's a

command, but I can hear the plea in her voice.

"Something nicer to hear?" I let a chuckle leave me with the question in an attempt to ease her.

"No, doesn't have to be nice. Just something more about you." The fire sparks beside us as I look down at her. Her bare chest presses against mine and I drink her in. The goodness of her, the softness of her expression.

"Hal, the man I killed... he hurt Angie. You heard me mention her before."

The mention of another woman's name makes her pause and I remind her, "She wasn't mine and I didn't want her like that, but I've always felt responsible for what happened."

"What happened to her?" She doesn't blink as she whispers her question staring into the fire.

"She came and went when we first... opened the club... she was one of our regulars on the weekends. Buying whatever she wanted to party with her friends."

"Drugs?" Bethany asks and I nod, waiting for judgment but none comes.

"One day she came to the bar on a weekday. I thought it was odd. She was dressed all in black and her makeup was smudged around her eyes. She wanted something hard. That's what she asked for, 'something hard.'" The memory plays itself in the fire and brings with it a hollowness in my chest.

"I told her to get a drink, but she demanded something else. So I told her no. I sent her away."

"Why?"

"I thought she would have regretted it. She'd just come from her father's funeral. There was nothing I had that would take that pain away and I knew she'd chase it with something stronger when it didn't work. She went to someone else. And I regret sending her away. I wish I could take it back. I wish I could take a lot of it back. By the time I saw her again, she'd changed and done things she didn't want to live with anymore. She was so far gone… and I'm the one who watched her walk away and sent her to someone else. Someone who didn't care and didn't mind if she became a shell of a person who regretted everything."

"You tried to help her. You can't be sorry about that." Bethany's adamant although sorrow lingers in her cadence.

"I can still be sorry about it, cailín tine," I whisper the truth as I brush her hair back. "And I am. I'm sorry about a lot of things. Mistakes in this world are costly. I've made more than my share of them."

"That doesn't make you a bad man," she whispers against my skin, rubbing soothing strokes down my arm, desperate to console me.

"You remind me a little of her in a way," I admit to her. "She was a good person. Angie was good, what I knew of her. She was good but sometimes dabbled in the bad and was able to walk away. I needed her to be able to walk away. To go back to everything and be just fine. To still be good. It made me feel like it was fine. I thought what we were doing was fine; that it was a necessary evil. It's simply something that's inevitable and something we'd rather control than give to someone else. But it's not fine and it never will be."

Bethany asks, "You think I'm a good person, dabbling in the bad?" Her voice chokes and she refuses to look at me even when I cup her chin.

"It's the same with you. I'm not comparing you to her. She's nothing compared to you but the good. You have so much good in you. Even if you cuss up a storm when you're mad and try to shoot strangers."

The small joke at least makes her laugh a small feminine sound between her sniffling.

"I'm not willing to let you go though—I'm afraid you'll never come back to me. Or worse, that you won't be able to go back to the good."

"You are not bad," she says and her words come out hard which is at odds with the tears in her eyes.

"I'm not good, Bethany. We both know it."

"And I'm not all good either. In fact, there are a lot of people out there who would tell you I'm a bitter bitch and they hate me," she attempts to joke, but it comes out with too much emotion. "You don't have to know if I'll still be good if I walk away, Jase. I don't want to walk away. And we can be each other's goods and bads. People are supposed to be a mix of both, I think. You need that in the world, don't you? You are needed," she emphasizes, not waiting for my answer. "And I need you," she whispers with desperation.

"I'm right here," I comfort her and she lets me hold her, clinging to me as if I'm going to leave her.

It's quiet as she calms herself down and I think she's gone to sleep after a while, but then she asks, "Is this... is this cards or bricks for you?"

"I don't understand."

"I'm insecure and I need to know. It's one of the bad parts of me. I'm insecure."

"You need to know... cards or bricks?" I ask, still not understanding.

"There are two kinds of relationships. The first is like a house built of cards; it's fun, but you know it's going to fall down eventually. Or you can have a house made of bricks. Bricks don't fall. Sometimes they're a little rough and it takes time to get them right, but they don't fall down. They're not supposed to anyway--"

"Bricks." I stop her rambling with the single word. "I'm not interested in cards. I don't have time for games."

"Then why lie to me?" She whispers the question with a pained expression. With her hand on my chest, she looks into my eyes. "I don't want to fight; I just want to understand."

"I kept you a few steps behind me. That's how I saw it. Not because I didn't trust you—I didn't trust that the information I had wouldn't hurt you. I didn't want to give you false hope."

She's quiet, and I don't know if she believes me. "Please. Trust me."

"I do. I trust you." At the same time she answers me, my phone pings from where I left it in the pile of clothes.

Bethany doesn't object to me leaving her to answer it. Although she watches intently, waiting for me to come back to her.

Reading the message Carter sent, I try to keep my expression neutral and tell her, "I have to go."

"You do that a lot," she comments before I bend down to give her a goodbye kiss.

"I'm sorry."

"Don't be. I'm right here. I'll always be here." A warmth settles through me with her whispered words.

"Is it going to be okay?" she asks, not hiding her worry.

"As okay as it ever is," I answer her truthfully. "We may know where Jenny is," I tell her and watch as she braces herself from the statement. "We're going to find her tonight."

"Jase, I love you," she whispers. "Make sure you come back to me. I'm not done fighting with you yet." A sad smile attempts to show, masking her worry, although it only makes her look that much more beautiful.

"I look forward to coming back here so you can yell at me some more," I say to play along with her, leaving a gentle kiss against her lips. When I pull back her eyes are still closed, her fist gripping my shirt like she doesn't want to let go.

"I'll come back." I swallow thickly and promise her, "I'll come back."

CHAPTER 18

Jase

There's a bridge that looks over the ferry. It leads to the docks where our shipments come in. With my brothers behind me and Seth next to me, we stare at the worn door that lies beneath the bridge.

It's made of steel and looks like it's been here as long as the bridge has; the shrubbery simply obscured it.

"We still don't know what's inside," Sebastian comments.

"Jenny," I answer. "I know she's in there." I can feel it in my bones that we're closer to where we're supposed to be. Even in the pitch-black night, with the cold settling into every crevice, we're close. I know we are.

"Let's hope so." Carter's deep voice is spoken lowly as he steps next to me, facing the bridge and considering the possibilities.

"Ten men?" I ask Carter, looking over my shoulder at the rows of black SUVs parked in a line. "Do they know?"

"They know we need them here and that's all. They're waiting for orders."

"Ten of them?" Seth repeats my question.

"Do you think that's overkill?" Carter questions in return. It's just the four of us, me and Seth and him and Sebastian, along with our ten men. Daniel and Declan are home with guards of their own. Just in case anyone sees us leaving as an opening to hit us where it hurts. In this life, there is never a moment for weakness and having someone you love at home is exactly that, a weakness waiting to be exploited.

"I don't know if it'll be enough," Sebastian answers. His hand hasn't left his gun since we got out of the car. He's ready for war and prepared for the worst. He knows what it's like to be given an order by Marcus better than any of us. By the way he's acting it looks like he expects each of our names to be on a hit list given to Marcus's army.

"It wasn't supposed to turn into this. It should have been low key." Seth looks concerned as he searches the edge of the bridge for signs of anyone watching or waiting. "He has eyes everywhere."

"If Marcus wants to kill us, I imagine he could do it with no men," I tell the group who have gathered around us.

"We're walking underground with no concept of what's there."

"Explosives would do it," I say, completing the thought that lingers in the back of my mind.

"You think he knows?" Carter asks.

"I think we should assume he does," Seth answers.

"If he didn't before we got here, he does now." The realization hits me hard. "All of us can't go in there. This was a mistake."

"What the hell are you talking about?" Carter snaps.

"There are too many questions unanswered. If we all go in, he could see it as either us declaring war or an opportunity... We can't give him the opportunity. He can know war is coming though."

"We go in together," Carter insists as I grip my gun tighter, feeling my palm get hot with the need to do something.

"Think about Aria." I try to persuade him to go back home.

"I am. I'm thinking about my family and about bringing them home. Open up the fucking door."

"Don't leave her a widow," I warn him. "Not for me."

"She knows what I'm doing. She knows the risk." I can only nod, thinking that Bethany knows the same. Carter adds, "She told me not to come home without Bethany's sister. She knows and she wants Jenny home too. Open it." With the command and the four of us moving forward, the men gather behind us, all of us walking to the small door.

With a gun trained on the lock, Sebastian fires and a flash of light and red sparks from the gun being shot leads to the groan of the heavy door being opened. Sebastian steps aside and only nods as we move forward. His eyes are focused straight ahead as he orders the men around us, keeping a lookout and moving forward to clear the way.

"I'll go in first," I tell him, stepping in front and preparing myself for what we'll find.

The steel floors grate as I step forward, letting my eyes adjust and not daring to breathe. The musk of the water's edge is heavier when the door opens. A steel rail keeps me from stepping forward and it's then I notice the door leads to a spiral staircase down. It reminds me of the shed at The Red Room. The place men go to die but unlike them, we're walking down there willingly. A cold prick flows down my skin like needles.

"We don't have a choice." Carter pushes the words through clenched teeth before I can urge him to turn around.

"This is my fight," I tell him one last time.

"We fight together." The weight against me feels more significant than it ever has before. "Bastian," I call before taking another step forward. "Don't let a single man here die."

He tells me simply and then motioning with his chin for me to continue, "I wasn't planning on it. In and out. No casualties."

With a nod and a look back at Carter and Seth, I take the stairs one at a time, noting how many there are and how far down it goes. Maybe two stories, if that. It's got to be twenty feet down and the steady drip from leaking pipes is all that makes a noise down here.

Four men stay at the top and just outside the door as lookouts. The rest join us, making it ten men in a tight space, eight of them waiting on the stairs for the door at the bottom to be opened.

Bang!

It takes a second shot to shatter the lock and I toss it to the floor before slowly pushing open the door. Seth's behind me, his gun raised and ready. Steadying my breathing, focusing on my racing pulse, I take in every inch that I can see.

There's no sign of anyone. No sign of anything at all down here. Anxiousness makes me doubt myself. Maybe she's not here at all. With that thought, unexpectedly the lights turn on, one after the next, quickly illuminating the place.

The sound of guns cocking and raising fills the tight space, but no one fires. The lights are newer than everything else. They're placed into sconces bracketed against the walls which are a mix of thin plaster and tightly packed dirt.

"Electric," Seth notes. "Someone was hired to install these," he says and I can already see the wheels spinning.

"Look for a paper trail when we get back," I tell him, leading the way further into the unknown territory. "If Marcus hired someone, they may have seen him or someone who has."

"Already noted."

I have to stop before I get more than five feet in; there are so many rooms, so many branching paths. "It's almost like a mine the way it's built with a maze of halls."

"Where do we start?" Seth asks. His expression appears overwhelmed as he moves his gaze from one hall to the next. All open doors, and all could lead to armed men or worse.

My brother comes up behind us, considering everything carefully. All the while I hear the tick of a clock in my head.

"It could take hours." The second the words slip out of my mouth, I hear a skittering in the dirt.

A scraggly boy, thin but tall with lean muscle watches from the shadows to the left. The second I spot him, he takes off. My gun lifts first, instinctively ready, but he's unarmed and I can hear his footsteps getting farther away.

"Left," I yell out and chase after him. He's the build of the kid who left the note on Carter's windshield. "He works for Marcus." My lungs scream as I chase after the kid, rounding a hall and barely spotting him through another. Seth's right at my heels and the men behind him spread out, watching each door. Careful and meticulous, not reckless like the man in front has to be.

The need to find this kid, to stop him rages hard inside as I race through the underground, chasing after the sound of him running. He may know where she is. He'll know what this place is at least.

I can hear them all behind me as Seth and I take the hall carefully, checking doors as we go.

My lungs squeeze and I struggle to breathe in the damp air as I lose the sound of him first. Then I lose sight of him with the sconces slowly flickering off and on.

It's my worst nightmare. Trapped in a small space with everything riding on this moment and yet I have no answers and it's all slipping away.

I don't stop running, searching every corner with Seth and listening intently, only to run into a sign. A sign that stops both of us in our tracks. The sign the kid led us to.

Four lines are written on a board blocking the hall. The boy is nowhere to be seen although the click of a door sounds in the far-off distance.

Leave the boy.
All those who made a deal with Walsh can enter.
Everyone else leave now.
Or the girl dies.

"What happened?" Carter questions in a hushed demand as he comes up behind me. My heart's racing, my palms are sweaty. He knew. Marcus knew and let us come.

"You have to go," I answer him as I take in a deep inhale, feeling my pulse pump harder. I can't lift my eyes from the sign. "Or the girl dies."

She can't die. Bethany needs her.

"He knew we were coming," I speak loud enough for all of them to hear as they make their way into the space. "Get them out," I tell Sebastian. "Get everyone out!" I have to raise my voice so Sebastian can hear.

"He wants us to know he knows and to admit it," Seth speaks out loud, referring to the deal with Walsh.

"Admit it in front of our men," Carter adds, looking behind him at the men lined up and ready to fight beside us. Ready to die for us.

"I couldn't give two shits who knows." My hiss of a mutter grabs his attention and I look him in the eyes and tell my brother, "I promised Bethany I'd bring her sister back." The thumping in my chest rages. "Even if I have to go in alone."

"I'm here, Jase," Seth speaks up, reminding me I'm not alone.

Carter speaks before I can answer, "Then do it." He doesn't let go of me, he grips my arm and forces me to stand there a second longer. "Don't get yourself killed." He says it like it's a demand, but it's drenched with emotion.

"And to think, I was expecting you to tell me you love me," I joke back in a deadpan voice even though dread consumes me. It's just to ease the tension and hurt that riddle every muscle inside of me at the thought of Jenny being dead already and Marcus being one step ahead as usual. Merely toying with us.

"That too," Carter adds.

With a farewell grip on his shoulder, I look him in the eyes and tell him, "I'll try not to be stupid."

"Go," he tells me and shares a glance with Sebastian. With a nod of his head, Sebastian starts to lead the men back.

"I'll see you when it's through," I answer Carter as he walks off without looking back.

"You should go too," I tell Seth as the place empties. "Go with them."

"What are you talking about?" His voice is low with disbelief.

"You stay back. In case it's a setup." I can feel chills flowing down my skin at the thought of Marcus being more prepared than we are. He's the one who made the rules to this game. He knows it better than anyone. He sets himself up to win.

"I'm the one who needs to go in. I'm the one who brought us all here." A cold sweat breaks out across my shoulders and down my back before taking over my entire body as I stare down the barren hall. It feels like my death sentence. I'm a fool to think otherwise, but I have to go in. I can't leave her here. I can't and I won't.

"It says 'all,'" Seth says as he looks me in the eyes, defying me and referring to the sign that blocks the path. "I'm not letting you go in there alone." Disregarding my orders he takes a step forward, pushing the sign to the side, into the dimly lit hall and I yank him back, fisting the thin white cotton of his shirt.

Time passes with both of us waiting for the other, knowing what we're walking into and looking it in the eyes anyway.

"Are you sure?" I ask him.

"We're in this together. I have to admit, I didn't really care for Marcus before, but now I hate the fucker." He offers me a hint of a smirk and a huff of humor leaves me. Patting his back, I grip my gun with both hands. He readies his and I nod.

"We get her and we get out."

"Got it," he says then nods and we go in together.

The thumping in my chest gets harder listening to Seth's pace picking up to match mine as we move down the dark hall, the smell of soil and rust filling my lungs as we move.

"You have a strong family," Seth comments with something that sounds like longing.

"We're close," I answer him and he glances at me, but doesn't say another word.

"Let's not die today. I'd like to go back to them."

CHAPTER 19

Bethany

I CAN'T GET THIS FEELING OUT OF THE PIT OF MY stomach.

Sitting and waiting. Sitting and waiting. I don't like sitting and fucking waiting around.

Everyone you love will die before you. My mother's voice has kept me company for more hours than I can count. Warning me. I let myself fall and it feels like I've been delivered a death sentence. Why did I let myself fall? Why did he have to keep me from running?

The thump of the book falling from my hand down to the floor scares the shit out of me. My nerves are messier than ever; they're worse than a necklace tangled at the bottom of a luggage case on a bumpy road trip.

I force myself to read The Coverless Book. I read every page in it. I read about Emmy feeling better and the two of them getting married in secret. I read about them falling in love and sharing their first time together.

Then a new sentence started as he watched her lie down, but I don't know how it ends. I stared at the last page for the longest time, not understanding. It's half a sentence, mid-thought from Jacob about how he'd do anything for her. Someone cut the pages out. Lots of them. It looks like there's at least twenty missing that I can spot. So much for reading to distract me.

I know there's more to the story. It can't be cut short like that. The moment the thought hits me, I'm drenched in the nightmare of my sister crying on the floor. Telling me she just wanted them to have a happy ending.

"Jenny," I breathe her name, staring at the clock and wanting Jase to come back with her.

I can't sit here and do nothing.

With nothing to distract me, my mind goes to the worst of places. Pacing and staring into the fire as the smell of leather envelops me.

Dropping my hands to my knees, I feel the flames as my hair hits my face. It's the waiting that kills me. I can't sleep without seeing my mother remind me that *everyone I love will die before me.* I can't think without wondering if Jase has found Jenny and all the things she may have had to endure. I don't know who she'll be when he finds her. *If* he finds her.

This isn't a way to live, waiting and in fear.

Are you there? I text Laura and wait. I'm exhausted from barely sleeping, but there's no way I can sleep now.

I'm scared, I message her again, needing to tell someone. She doesn't text me back though. She could be working; she could be sleeping. I don't know. I don't know anything anymore.

"Fuck this," I say then toss the book down on the table and make my way out of the room. The hall seems longer than it has before as I head for the grand staircase and the hidden door beneath it.

My pulse pounds in my temples as I place my hand on the scanner to open it. It takes a long moment. "Please open," I whisper as the jitters flow through me.

It does, the large door slides aside seamlessly, presenting me with a dark kitchen until I turn the lights on.

It's empty and quiet. The whole world is sleeping while mine crumbles around me. A sudden chill overwhelms me and a split second later the click of the heater makes me jump.

"Carter," I call out as I walk deeper into the kitchen. My feet pad on the floor and that's the only sound other than my racing heart. Something's wrong. I can feel it in my bones.

Wrapping my arms around myself I make my way to the other hall that the kitchen leads to. It's quiet and dark.

"Anyone," I call out and my voice strays from me, receiving no answer. "I don't want to be alone right now." It's a hard feeling to accept, when you open yourself up to love and then feel fate toying with taking them from you. "I don't want to be alone anymore."

"Bethany?" a voice calls out just as I turn on my heel to walk away.

"Daniel?" I question, fairly sure it's him and not Jase's other brother. Someone's here at least. "Were you sleeping? I'm sorry, I hope I didn't wake you up." The sentences tumble from my mouth as he makes his way into the kitchen, also in bare feet and gray pajama bottoms with a white t-shirt tight over his chest. He has to pull it the rest of the way down as he stops at the counter.

"No, you're fine, I was just lying down with Addison but not sleeping." There are bags under his eyes, so I know he's tired. "You okay?"

"Are you?" I ask him, feeling the anxiousness grip my throat.

His expression softens to a knowing look. "It's hard. Moments like this can be difficult," he admits and just to hear someone else say what I feel is a slight relief.

"I don't know how to be okay right now." Gripping the tips of my fingers to have something to hold, I watch as he pulls out a wine glass and then heads to the cellar.

"Do you like white or red?" he asks and I swallow a small laugh at the implication that the answer is to drink. "Red."

It's quiet as he opens the bottle, the dim light from outside glinting off the torn metal wrapper.

"I don't know what I can do to help." I emphasize the last word as he gently pushes the glass toward me and then pours one for himself.

He doesn't answer me; instead he takes a drink and so I do the same, sipping on the decadent wine and feeling guilty that I can.

"I just have a bad feeling," I finally confess. "It won't leave me alone and I'm afraid."

Daniel's still quiet, but he nods in understanding. I start to wonder if he'll speak at all until he says, "Let him do what he knows how to do, what he's good at."

"That doesn't--"

"Yes it does. You want to be involved," he says then looks me in the eyes and that's when I see the remorse in his. "You want to be there in case something happens." His voice drops as he tells me, "I know that feeling."

"I'm sorry."

"Don't be. I get to be here with Addison. Don't be sorry for me. There's nothing in this situation to be guilty or sorry or resentful over." He leans forward on the bar before looking over his shoulder down the empty hall. "We do what we're needed to do," he says with resolve.

"I don't know what I'm needed to do," I admit to him, feeling the weight lift, knowing that's the core of my problem in so many ways.

"When he brings your sister back, you take care of her. You're good at that, aren't you?"

The thought of Jenny being here soon forces me to brace myself on the counter.

"I heard that's what you do," Daniel prods, waiting for me to look back at him and I nod.

"Take care of her when she comes back, because that's something no one else can do. Let Jase do what he does and you do what you do."

"Even if I'm scared?" I question him in a whisper.

"Can I tell you a secret?" he asks and again I nod.

"We all are. Anyone who tells you they're not is lying. We live in a world where there's plenty to be afraid of. It's okay to be scared sometimes, but have hope. Have faith. Jase knows what he's doing."

CHAPTER 20

Jase

With single bulbs swinging slightly and creaking as they do from the high ceilings, the hall is dim. The rocking of the water can be felt in the aged corridors.

"How old is this place?" Seth murmurs his question as he gently kicks the first steel door open. Without a light in the small ten-by-ten room, it's hard to look in every corner. The rustling of Seth's shirt as he pulls out a small flashlight and clicks it on gets my attention. The heat of worry, of restlessness, is dulled by my conditioned response to chaos, *stay calm*. Always calm and alert. Or else death is sure to come for you.

He brings the light to his gun, both hands holding the pair steady and revealing an empty room inside. There's only a mattress on the floor and nothing else.

The same with the next room and the next.

Rows of doors, mostly open, line each side of the hall and we go through each one. Every door we open that reveals nothing but rumpled blankets and makeshift beds leaves me with the dreadful thought that we're too late… that when we push the next door open wider, it'll reveal a girl on the floor, no longer breathing.

"We can't be too late." The fear disguises itself as a hushed request.

"She's here," Seth reassures me beneath his breath as he turns the knob of the next door, and lets it creak open, revealing another barren room. "Why else would he do this?"

My gaze moves instinctively to him. "Why does Marcus do anything?"

"If you want to beat him, you have to think like him. Why this place? Why the boy? Why the sign?" He pauses to make sure I've heard.

"Why her in the first place?" I add to the pile of questions.

I count the remaining rooms, four of them, two on each side. Three open, one closed.

My mind travels to deceit. Wondering if he already took her away. Wondering if Marcus locked the two of us in here in her place. "If his intention was so easily known, he wouldn't be who he is."

With the slow creak of the next steel door, rusted on the bottom edge, I hear Marcus's rough laugh in my memory and an icy sensation flows over my skin. Unforgiving, cruel.

We betrayed him first. I can already hear his excuse.

We came onto his territory; we stole from him. The only question is: what are the consequences?

"Empty too," Seth whispers. The next room and the next prove the same.

Prepared to be left with nothing but more questions and curses hissed beneath our breath, I place my hand on the final closed door and turn the knob, but it doesn't move.

Seth and I share a glance in the silence as I try again and then quietly shake my head. *Locked.*

Hope thrums in my chest as my pulse races and I take one step back and then another.

"On the count of three?" Seth asks, backing up with me. Nodding, I tell him, "Kick it in."

One.

Two.

Three.

My muscles scream as I slam my boot against the door as hard as I can along with Seth, the two of us putting everything we have against the steel lock with the last hope of seeing Jennifer behind it.

The door slams open to reveal darkness and then a shriek. My eyes can't adjust fast enough, although I think I see her small form just before I hear the *bang!*

The heat of a gun going off, the metal against my skin, singeing my shirt and filling the air with the smell of metallic powder is disorienting but familiar. Adrenaline surges in my veins and I'm quick to push forward, not knowing if the bullet hit me, grazed me, or if I was spared from the shot. Anger, fear, and the need to survive all war inside of me to come out on top as I shove myself forward, closer to the gun and whoever's holding it.

Bang! It goes off again, the shot hitting the ceiling with a pop of steel breaking that joins the crackling of the plaster that falls from above my head.

My body hurtles forward, landing on top of the small woman who's desperate to cling to the gun. She fires it again as I grip the barrel, forcing it away from me just in time to send the shot wide and feeling the burning hot metal as I rip it from her hands and toss it away. It thuds on the floor as she turns under me, desperate to get it back.

"Jennifer!" I scream out her name and hear Seth cuss behind me.

She screams and kicks wildly, fighting like her life depends on it.

"Stop!" The command is torn from me with equal parts demand and desperation. Seth moves to the side, kicking the gun farther out of reach. "Stop fighting," I grit out as her heel hits my ribs and she scrambles on the dirt floor.

The impact to my ribs leaves me seething, the pain rocketing through me as I clench my teeth and hold on to her.

"I don't want to hurt you."

"Calm down," Seth demands lowly, and it comes with the faint sound of a gun being cocked. That gives her pause. "I don't want to hurt you either," he says calmly.

Jenny stops moving, stops fighting and her gaze moves to Seth in the darkness. I can barely see him, but I can see the glint of the gun.

Time moves slowly as I back away from her to stand and while I do, Seth lifts his gun the second she looks at him. He uncocks it. "I didn't want to do that," he admits to her, swallowing thickly. "Just calm down. We're here to help you."

It's only then that I can take a good look at her.

What's most alarming is how disoriented Jennifer is. She's not skin and bones like I thought she'd be. Even through the grime that covers her skin, she has weight to her that lets me know she's been eating. Her eyes though are dark with lack of sleep and fear drives every half step she takes as she backs away, trying to get away from us, but knowing the wall is behind her.

With her gaze darting from me, to the gun, to Seth, she crouches down and stares up at us, ready to scream and fight.

"We're here to help you." I keep my voice low as I speak. The ringing in my ears from the gun she just fired has dulled. All I can hear now is her ragged breathing.

Seth tells her calmly, lowering himself down with both hands in the air, "We're here to save you."

I do the same, raising my hands and letting her know, "We're not here to hurt you."

With wild eyes full of disbelief, she shakes her head, letting us know she doesn't believe us.

"I'm not leaving without you," I tell her and the thin girl shoves her weight against me and her ragged nails scratch down my neck. Seething in the slight pain and more pissed than anything, I snatch her wrists and hold her close. "Calm down."

"You're not taking me," she screams out. Even held close, she doesn't stop fighting. It's useless though. She has to know it, but she doesn't stop. Kicking out and wriggling to get away, she never lets up. Pressing her against the wall, I'm careful not to hurt her, just to keep her as still as I can until she can calm down.

"We're taking you to your sister." Seth has the common sense to bring up Bethany.

"Bethany asked us to save you," I tell her and add, "I told her I'd bring you back."

For the second time she stills, but I don't trust it. "To save me? Bethany?"

The mere mention of Bethany paralyzes her. With a gasp and then harsh intakes, Jennifer trembles and her body wracks with sobs. She tries to fight it, writhing in my embrace in an effort to cover her cries, but she breaks down instead. No longer fighting us, instead she wars with herself.

"It's okay," I say and rock her, but my eyes move to the gun on the floor and Seth's quick to take it.

"Where is she?"

Keeping my voice soft and soothing, I answer her. "We'll take you to her."

"Right now, okay?" Seth adds sympathetically, the way someone speaks to a lost child. I pull back slightly, giving Jennifer more space and taking my time to release her, still ready to pin her down again if I need to so she doesn't attack either of us or hurt herself in the process.

"We're going now; we'll take you right to her." The second I release her fully, her arms wrap around herself. Her sweater, once a light cream color judging by its appearance, is dirtied with brown.

"The note said it was time," she murmurs and looks away from us, rocking back and forth.

"Time for what?" Seth questions and I watch her. Her wide eyes are corrupted with fear and regret.

"It just said it was time and there was the gun. I

thought…" she trails off as the tears come back and the poor girl's body wracks with a dry heave. She braces herself with both palms on the ground.

"It's okay," I comfort her, rubbing her back and wondering how Bethany is going to react. How she'll be after seeing her after so long.

"What happened?" I have to ask. It's the first time I'm able to look around and the room is the same as the rest. My stomach drops low when she tells me she doesn't remember everything, but she's been in this room for as long as she can remember since she's left.

"This is where he kept you? Marcus put you in here?"

"I asked him to," she admits and her voice cracks. "I just don't remember why or what happened."

"We'll have a doctor come," I tell her, petting her hair and noting that it's clean. It's been washed recently.

"Did he touch you?" I ask her, needing to know what Marcus did. It's the only thought that comes to mind as I stare at the mattress on the floor.

With her disheveled blonde hair a matted mess down her back, she stares down at herself as if seeing her appearance for the first time. She shakes her head and answers in a tight voice, "He didn't." She's quick to add with a hint of desperation, "I want to see a doctor." "I need to know that I'm better."

"Better?"

Her dull eyes lift to meet mine and a chill threatens to linger on my skin, the room getting colder every second we stay here. "He said he'd help me get better if I helped him."

"What did you have to do?" Seth asks, but I cut her off before she can reply.

"We need to get out of here. Come with us," I urge her, feeling a need to get out as quickly as we can. The longer we stay here, the more we talk in Marcus's territory, the more tangled this problem will get.

I usher her to the door, reaching out for her, but she's quick to jump back, smacking her body against the cinder block wall although she doesn't seem to notice. She yells in the way a child does when they're scared and they need an excuse to keep them from having to walk down a dark hallway. "Wait."

Tears leak from the corners of her eyes and their path leaves a clean line down her mucky skin. "Is Bethany okay?" Her voice cracks and her expression crumbles as she holds herself tighter, but her eyes plead with me, wanting to know that everything's all right. "Tell me Bethany's okay… please?"

CHAPTER 21

Bethany

To know something is one thing. It's a piece of a thought, a fact, a quote. It stays in your head and that's all it will ever be. A nonphysical moment in your mind.

But to *see* it—or to see someone—to feel them, smell them, hear them call out your name... There is no replacement for what it does to you. How it changes you. It's not a piece of knowledge. That's life. Making new memories and sharing them with others. There is no way to feel more alive than to do just that.

Than to hold your crying sister, collapsed in your arms as tightly as you can hold her as she cries your name over and over again.

As I breathe in her hair, the faint smell of dirt clings to her, but so do childhood memories and a desperate need to hold on to her. To never let her go again. In any sense of the word.

"I'm so sorry," she murmurs, her breath warm in the crook of my neck as I hug her tighter to me, shaking my head. As if there's no room for apologies.

I don't want to tell her I'd given up. I don't want to tell her what's happened. I want to go back. Back to the very beginning and fight for her and never stop. If only time and memories worked like that.

"Are you okay?" I barely speak the question before a rustling behind her, toward the doorway to the guest bedroom catches my attention.

Jase is hovering, watching us and I wish he'd come in closer to hear. Jenny needs all the help she can get.

Jase clears his throat and speaks before Jenny can. "The doctor is on his way. She's having some minor--"

"I can't remember," my sister cuts Jase off. My gaze moves from his to hers although she won't look me in the eyes.

"I know I left, I know where I was, but the days… I don't remember, Bethy." Her shoulders hunch as her breathing becomes chaotic. The damage has been done. Whatever that damage may be.

"Hey, hey." Keeping my voice as soft and even as I can, I grip her hand and wait for her eyes to meet mine. "It's okay." The words are whispered, but they're true.

"You're here now. You're safe." Jase's voice is stronger, more confident and I thank the Lord for that.

"You remember me, and that's all that matters," I say without thinking. Instantly, I regret it.

"Mom didn't remember us." Jenny's words are lifeless on her tongue.

Digging my teeth into my lower lip, I watch Jase stalk to the corner of the room and take a seat on the edge of the guest bed. The room is still devoid of anything but simple furniture and curtains. It's exactly the same as it was when I was first here, only weeks ago.

It's only been short of a month, and yet so much has changed in the strongest of ways.

"You'll remember the days, or you won't. But it's because of what happened to you. Not because of you," I speak carefully, keeping in mind that Jenny's scared, and that I need to be strong for her.

Even though I feel like crumbling beside her.

Her eyes turn glossy as she sobs, "I'm so sorry I left. I'm sorry I ever left."

"I'm here," is all I can say. Over and over, I pet her hair to calm her and shush her all the while.

Jase is quiet, but there. If I need him, he's there. Gratitude is something I've never felt to this degree before. My life will be dedicated to making him feel the same.

A shower calms my sister. Maybe it's the comfort of the heat, or maybe it's washing away what she does remember. With both of us in the bathroom, her drying off and getting dressed and me staring at the door so as not to watch, I ask her, "What did Marcus do to you?"

The fear creeps up and then consumes me. Imagination is an awful thing and I wish I could stop it.

"I don't remember everything," she confesses. "I know I feel..." she trails off to swallow thickly and I prepare for the worst. Picking under my nails and steeling my composure, I ready myself with what to say back, putting all the right words in order to make her feel like she's all right now, as if there were ever such a combination.

"I feel healthier. More with it. I haven't had a… a need to."

"To what?"

"To take a hit." Her answer comes out tight and I turn to see her staring at me as strength and sorrowful memories are worn on her expression. "I feel better."

She breaks our gaze, maybe from the shame of what used to be, I don't know. I return to looking ahead as she dresses in a pair of my pajama pants and a t-shirt.

Better.

My bottom lip wobbles and I can't help it. I can't help how tense I feel. *Better.*

Of all the things, that's a word I would never have known would come from her.

"I don't know at what cost. The idea of him scares me, even if I don't remember. I know I changed my mind. I changed the deal."

"Even if you don't remember what someone said or what they did to you, you always remember how they made you feel."

The towel drops to the floor as she blurts out, "Marcus scares me, Bethany. He scares the hell out of me."

"Do you remember anything that he did?" I ask her again, this time beneath my breath. All she gives me is a shake of her head.

"I don't know. I don't think he's going to let me walk away though."

The conviction in my voice is enough to break the fixation of her fear. "Then he'll have to fight me to get to you."

A SINGLE TOUCH

With her glancing at the knob, I open the door and cool air greets us. It feels colder without her answering me. She heads out first and after looking at Jase, still in the chair, his phone in his hand she apologizes to him.

"What did you do?" I ask her as Jase tells her it's all right.

"I shot him," she tells me, and I can't help the huff of a laugh that leaves me, although it's short and doesn't carry much humor.

"What's so funny?" She stares at me as if I'm crazy.

"She shot me when she first saw me too," Jase answers for me.

Jenny doesn't answer; she doesn't respond although she nods in recognition. The bed creaks in protest as she sits on the end of it.

"Can we have a minute?" I ask Jase. "I just need to talk to her," I reason with him, but it's unneeded.

With a single nod, he moves to leave and I'm quick to close the distance between us and hug him from behind. He's so much taller and it's awkward at first, but he turns to face me and I rest my cheek against his chest, breathing in his scent and hugging him tighter. "Thank you," I whisper and feel the warmth of my air mix with his body heat.

There's something about the way he holds me back, his strong hand running soothing circles on my skin while his other arm braces and supports me. I could stand here forever, just holding him. But Jenny needs me.

I kiss his chest and he kisses my hair before we say goodbye.

I don't know what Jenny's seen or what she thinks as she's staring out of the window.

The bed dips as I sit down cross-legged behind her, watching Jenny intently and telling her that I'm here for her.

"I miss Mom," is all she says for the longest time. Other than her constant apologies. Sorry for letting me think she was missing and then that she was dead. She didn't think it would happen like this.

After every apology, I tell her it's all right, because truly it is. I only ever wanted her back. This doesn't happen in real life. You don't get to wish for your loved ones to come back and then they do.

"I'm just happy you're here." This time when I tell her, I reach my hand forward, palm upturned and she takes it.

"Me too," she tries to say, but her words are choked.

I struggle to find something else to talk about. Something to distract her, to make her feel better. Life has slowed down since she's left. Slowed down and sped up, a whirlwind of nothing but Jase Cross for me. And I'm not ready to share that story with her yet. It's too closely tied to me mourning her.

"Did you read the book?" she asks in the quiet air. Nothing else can be heard but the owls from outside the windows and far off in the forest. They're relentless as the sky turns dark and the end of winter makes its exit known.

"I did," I answer her and before I can tell her what I thought, she speaks.

"I hated the ending. I'm sorry, I ripped it out." I almost tell her I know. I almost say the words as she does. "I wanted them to have a happily ever after."

My blood turns to ice as the memory of her sobbing on the floor while she ripped out the pages comes back to me.

It was only a dream, I remind myself. Only a dream. It didn't really happen. But yet, the question, the question asking her if she did that is right there, waiting to be spoken.

A different one creeps out in its place. There was a line I could never forget. "Why did you cross out 'I hate you for giving me hope?'"

"It wasn't me," she answers me and the chill seeps deeper into my bones. "It was Mom. Mom left it for you. I don't know why she pulled off the cover, but I hated the ending, so I ripped out the pages."

Goosebumps don't appear then vanish, instead they come and stay as I remember the dream. My sister and Mom did always look so alike.

"When she died there was that stack of books. This one had a post-it on it instead of a cover. She left it for you, but I took it."

"Why?" I don't know how I can speak when as we sit here, all I can see is the woman in my terrors.

"She said, 'Only you would understand, Bethany.' It pissed me off," my sister admits. "I took it and wanted to read it. I had to know why... why it was always you."

The eerie feeling that's been coming and going comes over me again, clawing for attention and I can barely stand not to react to it.

Bringing my knees into my chest, I try to avoid it, to shake it off. "What was the ending?" I ask her although I already know. It was some kind of tragedy.

"She died," Jenny says and her voice is choked. "That night, their first and only night, she died because she was really sick and there was no way to save her." My sister's shoulders heave as she sobs.

"It's okay." I try to reassure her that it's only a book, but both of us know it's so much more. It's the last words our mother left us.

"Her mother killed herself. The last ten pages is the mother facing Miss Caroline and telling her she hated her for giving her any hope and making her wait longer to end it all."

"That's awful," I comment.

Jenny sucks in a deep steadying breath and says, "The book is awful. It's all about how the ones you love aren't supposed to die before you."

Chills play down my shoulders, like a gentle touch. "What?"

I hear my mother's voice. *Everyone you love will die before you.*

"That was the point, that the greatest tragedy is watching everyone you love die before you do," my sister tells me with disgust. "I hate the book. I hate that Mom left it. I hate even more that she said you'd understand. You don't, do you?" Her eyes beg me to agree with her and I do.

"I hate it too. Mom wasn't well." I use the excuse, but her words keep coming back to me. She thought my life was a tragedy. She hadn't met Jase though. She couldn't have known my life would take this turn. "She's wrong," I say more to myself than to Jenny, but she nods in agreement.

"Even if they die," she whispers before staring out of the window, "you still got to love them."

"Do you ever feel like she's with us?" I ask my sister, feeling the eyes of someone watching us, but not daring to look to my left, toward the bathroom. No one's there,

I already know that. But still, something inside of me doesn't want me to look.

"All the time. I can't sleep because of it."

The cold evaporates, the uneasiness settles. It's only me and Jenny and I'll be strong for her.

"We'll get you on a good sleep schedule. I promise everything will be all right." I would give her all the promises in the world right now to keep her safe. Safe from Marcus and the world beyond these doors. Safe from herself and the memories that haunt her.

"I think I know why," Jenny says offhandedly as if she didn't hear me, still staring out of the window.

"Why what?"

"Why she crossed it out..." She doesn't give me the answer until she realizes I'm staring at her, desperate for a reason. "It didn't belong there. Hope is the best thing you can give someone, second to love. If it wasn't there... the mom wouldn't have killed herself."

It's quiet for a long time. The memories of my sister hurting herself stare me in the face, daring me to mention them and beg Jenny to realize there's so much hope.

I cower at the thoughts, mostly because she squeezes my hand, and I'd like to think it's because she already knows.

"If I had known it was a tragedy, I wouldn't have read it," I admit to her and then question why my mother would think I'd understand this book better than my sister. Why she would leave that book just for me? She wasn't well though so there's no reasoning there.

"That's what you have when there's no hope... tragedy." Jenny's comment doesn't go unheard and I let the statement sit before speaking out loud.

Not really to her, more to myself.

"Hope is the opposite of tragedy. It's a glimmer of light in utter darkness. It isn't a long way of saying goodbye. It's knowing you never have to say it, because whoever's gone, is still with you. Always. That's what hope is."

"They really are. They're always with us," she remarks.

"That's what makes it hard to say goodbye."

"You don't have to say goodbye," she says softly, as if she's considered this a million times over.

"Then how can you ever get over it?" I ask her genuinely, thoughts of her disappearance, of Mom being laid to rest playing in my mind. "How do you get over the loneliness and the way you miss them all the time?"

"Get over it?" she asks with near shock—as if she's never thought of it that way—and I nod without conscious reason.

"How?"

"You can never get over it. Whether you say goodbye or not. Loss isn't something you get over." My sister isn't indignant, or hurt. She's simply matter of fact and the truth of it, I've never dared to consider. She looks me dead in the eyes and asks with nothing but compassion, "So why say goodbye? Why do it, when they're still here and you'll never get over it? Never."

CHAPTER 22

Jase

"I JUST NEED TO KNOW..." BETHANY'S VOICE IS desperate, a sound I'm not used to hearing from her unless she's under me. She hasn't laid down since I told her it's time to go to bed. I don't know how long it's been since she's slept. Instead, she sits wrapped in the covers, staring at the door.

"She's all right." My words intertwine with the sound of the comforter rustling as I lean closer to her and wrap my arm around her waist. I pull her closer to me, making her lean slightly so I can kiss her hair, but I don't move her. She'll move when she's ready. I can wait for that.

I'll wait for her.

"Tell me you'll protect her." She swallows hard after blurting out the words. Her eyes are wide and glossy. "Please. I'll do anything." As she speaks her last word cracks and the only thing I can hear is her thumping heart, running like mad in her chest.

"Of course I will. She's family now."

"Family?" she questions me as if it's a foreign word.

"Bricks, cailín tine. I was serious when I said it, and serious about marrying you… even if you aren't ready."

"You really are bringing bricks and not just to fence me in, huh?" I have to laugh at her playful response. More than that, I love that she smiles. Even if it's gentle and small, it's there.

It falls quickly, though, as her gaze moves behind me to the door.

With one arm resting over her midsection and her other hand cradling her elbow, Jenny looks lost and uncertain as she clears her throat.

"Are you okay?" Bethany's quick to question and rise from the bed.

"Sorry," she answers and almost turns to leave, but Bethany stops her. "Wait. What's wrong?"

I stay where I am. Observing and waiting. Waiting for Bethany to tell me what's needed. Whatever it is, I'll be ready.

"I didn't mean to intrude."

"You weren't," Bethany assures her. I have forever with Bethany, so forever can wait a moment.

"Can… can we talk?" Jenny asks Bethany, although she looks hesitantly at me.

"Of course." If Bethany is aware of Jenny's objection toward me listening, she doesn't show it. Instead she drags the bench at the end of the bed closer to the chair by the dresser and pats it, welcoming her to sit.

"If you want me to go," I speak up, "I can grab you something to eat while you two talk?"

Jenny's gaze flicks between the two of us before she shakes her head. "You've already given me dinner, and a place to sleep… and clothes." She goes on and the baggy long-sleeve shirt pools around her thin wrist. "I don't need anything else."

As I stand to go the bathroom and busy myself so they have some semblance of privacy, Jenny adds, "Thank you." A tight smile and a nod is given to Jenny, but Bethany reaches for my hand and squeezes it before I can walk away.

I nearly think she wants me to stay, but she releases me with a *thank you.*

My hand is still warm from her touch when I turn on the faucet. Even over the sound of the water splashing in the sink, I can hear Jenny asks her questions about me.

Does she trust me?
What is she doing with me?
And finally, does she love me?

All of which are answered with many words, but the first of them each time is yes.

"You led him to me," Bethany informs her sister and I remember the first time I saw her. Across the bar, my fiery girl, picking a fight with whoever she could because she was hurting and needed help. Fighting is all either of us knew.

I scrub my face, feeling the roughness along my jaw and listen intently even though I hadn't planned on eavesdropping.

"The only clues you gave me before you left were The

Red Room and the Cross brothers. So I went there, searching for you."

Opening the cabinet to get my razor and shaving cream, I grab the bottle of pills and stare at them until they fall from my hand into the bottom of the trashcan beneath the sink. The inhale I take is deep and cathartic, but it doesn't stop the twisted hurt that will always come when I think about that time in my life. I don't need the constant reminder though.

Gripping my razor, I use the back of my hand to close the cabinet door. Jenny's reflection is clear in the mirror. A disturbed look plays on her face when she tells Bethany, "Marcus told me to. He said to make sure you heard me say it."

Staring down at the rippling water, I listen to her explain that she's sorry. She's sorry for everything.

I don't shave. I don't move, other than bracing one hand on each side of the sink and staring down, wondering what Marcus planned, how he thought ahead and what he thought would happen.

It's not until Jenny says good night and I feel Bethany's hand on my back that I bring myself to look at Bethany in the mirror.

"You okay?" she whispers against my back and I almost tell her that I'm fine. Instead I answer, "I hate hearing his name."

"Marcus?" she asks and I nod.

"Seth will find him," she answers me and plants a small kiss on my back through my white t-shirt when I turn off the faucet.

She watches me as I dry my face and thanks me for giving her sister space.

The smile on my lips falters until she reaches out, grabbing my hand and kissing it.

"Isn't that what a man is supposed to do?" I toy with her. "Kneel and kiss the back of a lady's hand."

A glimmer of surprise filters in her eyes as she says, "I thought it's what ladies did to the knights? I thought they kissed the back of their hands when they saved them."

Even though I'm still, she moves, pushing herself between me and the sink and reaching up to kiss me. It's always the same with her. The first is quick and teasing and then she gives me what I need, deep and slow. As I groan into her mouth, she lets out a soft sigh of affection and balls my shirt in her fist, bringing me closer to her.

"So needy," I tell her, my voice low and playful before tugging her bottom lip between my teeth and then letting her go.

I move my hands from her hips to her ass and pick her up, loving the gasp and then the squeal she gives me when I toss her on our bed.

The air heats as I kick off my pants and watch her right herself on the bed, her gaze wandering down my body until I climb on the bed to join her.

With both of her hands in my hair and mine bracing me on the bed as I lean over her, forcing her to lie down, she kisses me with soft, quick kisses all over my lips. I smile as she does it, short pecks moving in a clockwise motion.

I lift my head to look down at her, to joke about what she's done. I stop myself though; there's nothing but seriousness in her gaze.

"Thank you for saving me, Jase."

"You saved me too, you know," I tell her as I pull my shirt off, knowing damn well she has.

She stares at me for an awkward moment and then looks down with a huff. "I don't know what to say."

Confusion takes over. "What do you mean?"

"I don't know what would mean more right now. That I love you. Or that I don't love you."

The short huff of a laugh leaves me with relief. *Thank fuck.*

"Let's stick with I love you from now on."

"Then I love you, Jase Cross. I love you with everything in me."

CHAPTER 23

Bethany

GOOD THINGS DON'T COME OFTEN. NOT FOR me. Not for most people. I'm aware of that. I get it. Life isn't meant to be a garden of roses.

I'm used to the thorns. I would even say I like them. They're predictable, when nothing else is.

The sound of the printer in Jase's office that isn't an office makes me jump. It's louder than I anticipated, and I anxiously look to the doorway.

He should be here soon.

Jenny's tucked away in her room. Some days are better than others, but overall she's better. She's better than she has been in a very long time. If only she could remember what happened over the past few months, I think she'd be like my old sister again. Or at least who that girl was supposed to be.

Before the paper can fall to the tray, I catch it and lift it up to look at the certificate. It's so simple and not as expensive as I thought it would be.

It's merely a sheet of paper with ink on it. But then again so are books, and they can be wielded like weapons. They can destroy people; they can give them hope too.

"There you are." Jase's deep voice greets me with a sensual need. I can already feel his warmth before he wraps his arms around my waist and pulls me into his chest. The paper clings to my front as I keep it from his prying eyes.

"What are you hiding from me?" he questions.

"No hiding anything anymore. Isn't that the deal?" I remind him, peeking around to not just see him, but to steal a quick kiss as well. I love it when he smirks at me.

With a lift of his chin he tells me, "Then show it."

I do so willingly, listening to the paper crinkle and watching his dark eyes as he reads each line.

"Marriage certificate?" It's a sin that he looks so handsome, even when he's confused.

"It's a certificate to get a marriage certificate. Like a gift card. I didn't know you could get one of these. You have to be there for it to actually be done and all," I explain to him. I thought this would be the best way to tell him that I want to marry him.

As he steps back, snagging the paper from me and then looking between it and me, nerves flow through every part of me.

"My answer is yes." In my mind, when I decided I'd do this, I said it confidently, playfully even, but the way the words came out now was hurried and with an anxiousness to hear his response.

Which he still hasn't given me.

"At least I answered you quickly," I tell him and pretend like my hands aren't trembling.

"You want to do this?" he asks me, his shoulders squared as he lowers the paper to the leather sofa and closes the space between us.

Reaching up to adjust the collar of his pressed white shirt, I tell him easily, as if he's said yes, "I don't want a big wedding."

"Are you proposing to me?" he finally says with a grin and the playfulness and the charm are obvious. This is the man I love.

Nodding, I fight back the prick at the back of my eyes and tell him, "I am. Are you saying yes?"

"I already asked you, though. You don't get to ask me now." He walks circles around me, making me spin slowly.

"You aren't exactly good at it, so I figured I should give it a shot." I'm just as playful with him as he is me, nipping his bottom lip and then kissing him. He deepens it, stopping where he is and splaying his hands against my lower back and shoulder.

When he breaks the kiss, he stares down at me. "Why?" he asks me, toying with me and my emotions instead of just ending it quickly.

"You have no mercy," I joke with him. "Are you not saying yes?" I can't even voice the word no right now.

He only stares down at me, waiting for a response with a smug look on his face.

"When I'm sad, I want you to be there because then I feel less sad. When I'm happy, I want you there because

I want you happy with me. I just want you there… and I want to be there for you. If you'll let me." Tears form but I blink them away.

"I'll let you," he whispers ruggedly as he lowers his lips to the dip in my throat, giving me a chance to breathe easy. And to breathe him in.

"That's not how you say 'yes,' Jase. Or how you make a girl feel secure," I tease him although my words are still a bit unsteady. He pulls back to look at me, both of his hands still on me as I add, "When she prints out a marriage certificate, you're supposed to say yes."

"What if I gave her something else instead?" he asks, reaching into his pocket. "What if it was a tit for tat and I asked her a question to answer her question." My eyes turn watery as he gets down on his knee and pulls out a small black velvet box.

"I have something for you."

I can barely speak. "Jase."

"I love the way you say my name," he tells me, holding the box in one hand and my left hand in his other.

"I realized when I asked you to marry me, I probably should have done it better. I thought you'd be more willing to say 'yes' if there was something in it for you. I didn't think about a ring or feel like a ring would be enough."

Tears are warm as they fall down my face and I sniffle before telling Jase, "You are enough, Jase. It baffles me how you don't see that." I have to sniffle again before I can tell him that I'll remind him of it every day for as long as he lives if that's what it takes.

"Will you marry me?" he finally asks, opening the box. I don't have time to even look at what's inside. I need to touch him more than look at his surprise. I need to hold him and for him to hold me.

"I love you, Jase." I breathe against his shoulder, letting my tears fall to the thin white fabric.

"Say yes, first," he answers in what should be a playful voice, but feels nervous.

"A million times yes. It's always been yes."

Sometimes you meet someone, although maybe *meet* isn't quite the right word. You don't even have to say hello for this to happen. You simply pass by them and everything in your world changes forever. Chills flow from where you imagine he'd kiss you in the crook of your neck, moving all the way down with only a single glance.

I know you know what I'm referring to. The moment when something inside of you ignites to life, recognizing the other half that's been gone for far too long.

It burns hot, destroying any hope that it's only a coincidence, and that life will go back to what it was. These moments are never forgotten.

That's only with a single glance.

I can tell you what a single touch will do. It will consume you and everything you thought you knew.

I felt all of this with Jase Cross, with every flicker of the flames that roared inside of me. I knew he'd be my downfall, and I was determined to be his just the same.

He deserves as much. To have every brick in his guarded walls brought to the ground and be left to turn into something more. I want nothing between us. Nothing but us. Even if that means this world will collapse around us and become a chaos I never imagined.

So long as I'm with him, so long as his touch is within reach, I would give everything else up.

That's the part that scared me in that first moment. Somewhere deep inside of me I knew I would be his. And I'll do it again and again. In this life and the next.

CHAPTER 24

Jase

You're welcome for your gift.
It was mine to give all along.

MARCUS'S HANDWRITING STARES BACK AT me until I crumple the small parchment into my hand.

He's had a hand in the details, but he's slipping. More of his intention is showing. It's contradictory and changes on a whim, but he's falling. I can feel it.

One small token won't save him from the consequences of his actions. Our enemies will fall one by one, as they should. Their names will be carved in stone long before I allow anyone I love to meet the same fate.

He's the one who chose to be our enemy. A gift won't change that.

Balling up the note, I think back on everything that's happened. Not just to me, but also to my brothers and to Sebastian. It all comes down to the simple fact that we found irresistible attractions. And all the while, Marcus knew. He used them against us. Each and every one of us.

Sometimes when people are in pain they push love away. Tossing the paper into the metal trashcan outside the old brick building, I think of Sebastian and how much he tried to resist.

Pain makes people go to extremes they know are wrong. Carter is proof of that. Sometimes all life will give you is only a tragedy, but if you have someone to love, someone to hold on to, like Daniel and Addison had each other, then life will go on.

We are only men. Not invincible heroes.

And Marcus is just the same.

He's in pain like all of us. In fear like we've all been in. The answer to finding him, to bringing him to his knees lies in the one thing we've given into that he hasn't.

The girl Officer Walsh can't get over. The girl who ties him and Marcus together...

That girl will make Marcus fall. I know she will.

Seth will find her. *He must.*

"What's wrong?" Bethany's voice carries through the warmth of the April sunshine as her heels click on the sidewalk. Slipping her hand into the pocket of her jacket, she looks up at me and I can't resist brushing the hair from her face to cup her chin in my hand.

Before I can lean down to kiss her, she grips my dress shirt at the buttons, fisting the fabric in her hands and bringing her lips to mine. Desire ignites and the burn from it diminishes any other thought, any other need.

That's how it happens. It's how love conquers. Boldly, without fear, and with a ruling flame that nothing can tame.

Her lips soften the second they meet mine. Her body presses against my own as well. With a hand on the small dip at her waist I pull her closer to me, leaving nothing between us.

It's only when she pulls back that I even dare to breathe.

"I want to kiss you like that forever," she whispers against my lips with her eyes still closed. When they open, she peeks up at me through her lashes and adds, "I want to take my kisses from you every damn day."

A low groan of approval rumbles up my chest as she twines her fingers through mine.

"Now tell me what's wrong."

"A little demanding, aren't you, cailín tine?" A pang of nervousness worms its way between us. Before it can do any damage, I tell her, "I'm considering Marcus's next move." I resist telling her the second piece, but only for a split second. With her lips parted to answer me, I cut her off with, "And ours."

She doesn't let go of my hands, but she takes a half step back, letting her head nod. Intensity, curiosity, even fear swirl in her gaze. All the while, I wait for what she'll say, what she'll do.

"If you need me I'm here," she finally answers.

"All I need is for you to follow me," I tell her and lower my lips to hers. Nipping her bottom lip, the small bit of tension wanes. She may not be involved in what I do, but she'll stay with me.

I know she will. Because she loves me and she knows how deeply I love her.

Moving my hand around her waist, I'll make sure she never forgets, never questions what I feel for her.

She won't go a day without knowing. Her head rests against my arm as we walk, her one hand holding mine, the other on top of our clasped hands.

"It's all going to be all right," she tells me, although she stares ahead, noting the *Rare Books* sign in the window which causes her brow to furrow.

The smell of old books is unique, and it engulfs us as we walk deeper into the aisle. The full shelves of worn and previously read books make rows, but the one shelf at the very back is the one she needs to see.

"What are we doing here?" she questions and lifts her gaze to mine, but I only squeeze her hand in response.

"Jase," Bethany pushes for more, practically hissing my name although her steps have picked up with a giddiness she can't hide, making me chuckle at her impatience.

When I come to a stop in front of the shelves, she brushes against me and steps forward. I watch her reaction to seeing the wall of thin cream pages.

"They don't have covers?" she whispers and reaches out, her fingers trailing down the fronts of them.

I watch as she swallows, her throat tensing and her lips turning down.

"These are the books with no covers. No titles. They're only stories."

Her eyes glaze over, as I'm sure the Coverless Book

comes back to her, a gift from her mother and so much more. We may forget words or details, but the way we feel never leaves our memories. I know that book scarred her in a way I can't imagine although I'm not sure why.

"I wanted to get you another one. A different story to take its place."

"We drove hours and hours to get a book?" she questions silently, her eyes beseeching me to explain why.

"This is the only place I found on the East Coast that carried unknown books-"

"I don't want to read another tragedy," she says and cuts me off. "I don't want to risk it."

"You're going to want to though, cailín tine."

A second passes and I swear I can hear her heart beating, waiting in limbo for more.

"These books all came from one person's home years ago. She collected stories that made her feel loved."

Bethany turns her attention back to the books, back to the stories I want her to read.

"I brought you here because they call this the aisle of hope."

CHAPTER 25

Seth

WITH HER LEGS CROSSED LIKE THAT, HER red skirt rides up higher. It draws my eye and as she clears her throat, noticing my wandering gaze, I let the smirk appear on my lips before carelessly covering it with my hand.

It's been too long since I've been this close to her, face to face. Too many years since she's sought me out.

My stubble is rough beneath my fingertips; it'll leave small scratches against her soft skin when I ravage her with the hunger I've had for so long.

"Did you hear what I said?" Laura asks. When she got into my car with Bethany, I could feel the waves of apprehension hidden in the silence, the lust that roared back to life when Bethany left us. And we made a deal.

"You said you wanted an exchange. You want to change the details of our deal."

A SINGLE TOUCH

Her doe eyes beg me to consider, and they hold a vulnerability that her tense curves fail to deliver. She grips both arms of the chair across from me as her chest rises and falls with a quickened pace. She can't hide the fear of coming back to this life. *Of coming back to me.*

As her bottom lip slips between her teeth, I note that she can't hide the desire either.

"I've wanted this for too long to consider your proposal," I tell her, spreading my legs wider and leaning forward in my office chair in the back room of the bar. My elbows rest on my knees as I lean closer to her, only inches away as I whisper, "You know what I want."

"I can give you something you want more," she speaks clearly, although her last words waver when her gaze drifts to my lips.

Lies. There's nothing I want more.

I would have told her that and meant it with every bone in my body, but then she tells me, "I can give you Marcus."

ABOUT THE AUTHOR

Thank you so much for reading my romances. I'm just a stay at home mom and avid reader turned author and I couldn't be happier.

I hope you love my books as much as I do!

> More by Willow Winters
> www.willowwinterswrites.com/books